ROYALS AND RUSES

Weary Dragon Inn
BOOK TEN

S. Usher Evans

Sun's Golden Ray
Publishing

Pensacola, FL

Version Date: 10/13/24

© 2024 S. Usher Evans

ISBN: 978-0578920900

Map created by Luke Beaber of Stardust Book Services
Line Editing by Danielle Fine, By Definition Editing

Sun's Golden Ray Publishing
Pensacola, FL
www.sgr-pub.com

For ordering information, please visit
www.sgr-pub.com/orders

Other books in the
Weary Dragon Inn Series

Ale and Amnesia *(Newsletter Exclusive)*

Drinks and Sinkholes

Fiends and Festivals

Secrets and Snowflakes

Beasts and Baking

Magic and Molemen

Veils and Villains

Zealots and Zeniths

Campaigns and Curses

Perils and Potions

Royals and Ruses

Dearest cozy reader,

Because this is a cozy book, and so many of you are looking for escape from the usual fare of high stakes, I wanted to warn you that for a portion of this book, certain people and dog-like laelaps go missing. Rest assured, everyone is safe and will be reunited at the end.

I also wanted to warn that while the focus of the book is still cozy, there are some slightly higher stakes to work toward a satisfying conclusion for the series. But again, the affected citizens of Pigsend are quite safe, and everything will be resolved with a happy ending.

Thank you for going on this journey with me!

~ Sush

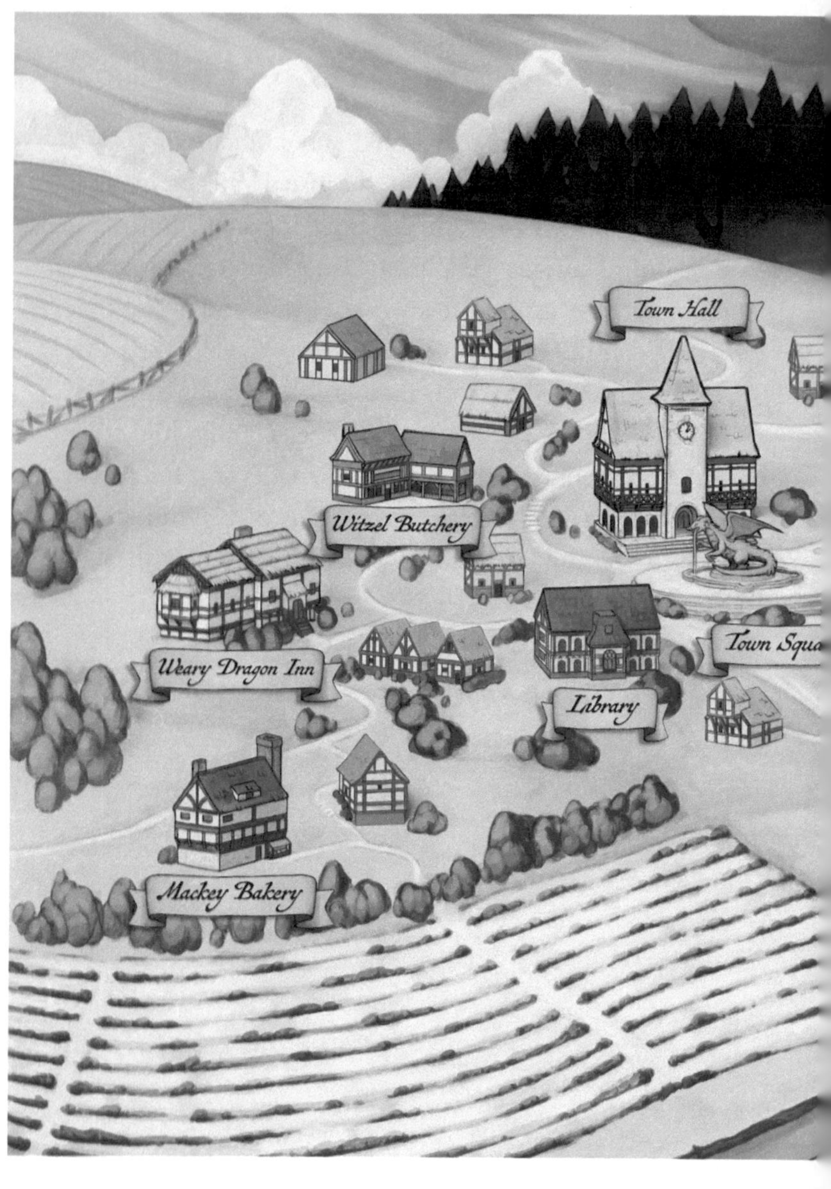

Town Hall
Witzel Butchery
Weary Dragon Inn
Town Squa[re]
Library
Mackey Bakery

Pigsend Tea Shop
Flour Mill
Pigsend Village

Chapter One

"I'm sorry… Did you say the *queen* is coming to Pigsend for the Harvest Festival?"

Bev stared at Mayor Jo Hendry with a buzzing between her ears. Around the table at the Weary Dragon, Ida Witzel and Lillie Dean wore the same look of absolute shock. Former sheriff Rustin furrowed his brow.

Hendry, even, looked surprised at her own words but forced a smile. "Yes, as I understand it, she will be paying our wonderful little town a visit."

Bev sat back, her mind whirring. "I don't… What in the…?"

"And *how long have you known that*?" Ida erupted, her cheeks darkening with fury. "I *knew* you were hiding something, Hendry."

"Not *hiding*," Hendry said. "With the queen, one never knows if something's going to happen until it's imminent. I didn't share it, because I didn't want the town to get up in arms until there was something to get up in arms about. Not only that, but with all the magical mishaps we've been having, I wasn't sure if Her Majesty thought it safe to be here." She cleared her throat. "In any case, I found out this morning. She *will* be here for the festival."

"But why?" Lillie asked, sharing a confused look with Bev. "She's the queen. What would she want with a Pigsend Harvest Festival?"

"I don't know," Hendry said. "But the facts are the facts. And we need to prepare for it."

"Would've been nice to have started preparing for this weeks ago," Ida said. As the Harvest Festival chair, she was in charge of all the moving pieces to get the event started and running smoothly. "But yes. Where's she going to be staying?" She looked around. "Here?"

"Goodness, I hope not," Bev said, earning a look of surprise from everyone at the table. "I don't have room. There are twelve beds, six rooms. Every one's been spoken for. I'd have to write loads of letters to the guests, and—"

"You won't have to do a thing," Hendry said. "She travels with a large entourage who bring tents and finery and whatever else Her Majesty needs to exist on a day-to-day basis. All they require is an empty field, so I'm sure one of the farmers would be happy to offer that up."

"Better make sure it's one who doesn't hate the queen," Ida muttered, sitting back.

"Yes, we'll be sure to skip the Silvers," Hendry said. "Maybe someone west of town? Alice or Herman or…well, certainly not Bathilda."

"No, certainly not," Bev said. Who knew what sort of magical creature Bathilda was hiding now? "I'm sure Alice would be happy to. Herman might worry about his pumpkins."

"Grant Klose could be an option, too," Ida said. "I'm not sure where his loyalties lie, but he's probably got a field he's done with for the winter."

"I'm sorry, can we come back to the fact that *Queen Meandra* is coming to *Pigsend*?" Lillie said, after a moment. "This makes very little sense. The town is so small, it's barely on a map. Why would she have business here?"

"I'll have you know our Harvest Festival is quite well-known," Ida said with a glare. "I'm not surprised it's attracted her attention. Especially with all the rules and regulations she put in place."

"I thought she just liked to have rules," Bev said mildly. "Rules about elections, rules about Harvest Festivals. Rules about how much wheat can be sold in Middleburg."

"I understand it's quite jarring, Lillie," Hendry said, patting Lillie on the top of the hand. "And a little worrisome. But we're going to push on as we have. The Harvest Festival is starting in two weeks, and there's lots to do." She rose. "Now, unless anyone else fancies a walk around town, I'm going to visit our farmers to find a suitable spot for Her Majesty's tent."

She walked out the door, leaving Lillie, Rustin, Ida, and Bev to stare at each other in stunned silence.

Rustin was the next to rise. "I'm going to…go home and lie down," he said. "Still not quite right after…"

Not a few days before, he'd been fired by another member of the queen's service, Karolina Hunter, for failing to notice Bernard the apothecary had been using magic. Bev didn't think Rustin had ever done his job well, but she still didn't like the idea of Karolina dismissing him. Or the fact that the soldier herself had decided to stick around and take his place until—

Bev snapped her fingers. "That's what Karolina was talking about."

"What?" Ida and Lillie said in unison.

"Karolina said she was staying in town to ensure the Harvest Festival went off without a hitch," Bev said. "She knew the queen was coming."

Rustin's face screwed up. "Oh, that confounded

woman—"

"Erm, never mind," Bev said.

"I'll walk you home," Ida said. "Do you have tea at your house? Get you a nice cuppa to settle in. We need our head of security at peak performance."

"Do you still want me after..." A big, fat tear leaked down his face. "After I was..."

"Yes, Rustin," Ida said emphatically, looking to Bev and Lillie for support. "You are an integral part of our planning committee. And you know this town better than Karolina. I'm sure her presence will be necessary to keep things...well, running smoothly. But we always need you."

"Y-yes," Bev said, with some difficulty. "We need you."

"Of course," Lillie, who, being newer to town, was able to lie better. "Go home and rest up. We'll see you for the meeting tomorrow."

Rustin smiled, the first one Bev had seen since his sacking, and left with Ida.

Bev exhaled and sat back, covering her face with her hands. "Goodness me. What a revelation."

"Bev, I...I'm scared," Lillie whispered.

Bev removed her hands and stared at her. Lillie's round eyes were wide and fearful, and she'd worried her bottom lip to the point that it was turning red. As a pobyd, a magical creature on Her Majesty's illegal list, Lillie had spent the majority of the queen's reign living in Lower Pigsend, a secret magical enclave not far from town. But after almost destroying the protective spell that kept it hidden, she'd been kicked out and had been rebuilding her life up here without causing much fuss.

"The queen? Here?" Lillie shook her head. "What do you think it means?"

Bev honestly didn't know. There were plans and machinations afoot, the most recent of which was a carefully orchestrated plot to have Rustin fired. That had worked, but Karolina staying in his place…that certainly wasn't what Andres Rade had intended, was it?

"I haven't a clue," Bev said. "Honestly, Lillie, I've seen hints the past few weeks about it, but never in my wildest dreams did I think…"

Lillie released her lip. "I should've sent that letter to Mr. Abora already. I'm sure the queen won't be coming to Silverkeep. No Harvest Festivals there—"

"Take a breath, Lillie," Bev said gently. "Let's not jump to conclusions until we've got all the information. Silverkeep's still part of the queen's domain, remember?"

"I suppose you're right," Lillie said. "I just thought Pigsend, being so small, was safer. Fewer eyes on us here. But the queen!" She exhaled a shaky breath. "Goodness, it's a shame Bernard's gone. Could use one of those calming draughts. A real one, not these dinky ones without magic."

"Suppose you could ask Merv to get one for you," Bev said. "I've half a mind to go down there myself and ask him about..." She stopped, remembering Lillie didn't know about the frame job Andres had orchestrated.

But she'd said enough.

"Bernard's in Lower Pigsend?" Lillie furrowed her brow.

"Yes, but obviously don't be spreading that around," Bev said. "It's quite a long, involved story, and the particulars of it aren't very... Well, let's just say there are some folks in Pigsend I no longer think that highly of." She shook her head. "But there was a goal in mind with those curses. It was achieved. The cursing stopped. That's really all that's important, I suppose."

"And now we've got the queen to worry about anyway," Lillie said, rising. "Well, I'm glad to hear Bernard's safe. I didn't buy that he was the culprit. After all, they were curses, weren't they? Bernard certainly wasn't cursing people. He didn't have any magical ability like that."

"Get some rest, Lillie," was all Bev could say.

In no time at all, the entire town knew about Her Majesty's impending visit. Bev had a stream of visitors that afternoon, including Allen Mackey, who worked with Lillie next door, and Pip Norris and his wife Holly, whose son was a dragon shifter who'd moved to the town of Sheepsburg to avoid crises like this. Bev offered the same neutral platitudes—she hadn't a clue why the queen had chosen Pigsend now—but kept a watchful eye on the butcher shop across the street.

Ida's wife Vellora was the one who'd originally invited Andres Rade, her former commander, to town. He'd been a high-ranking kingside officer and was apparently building support for some unknown cause. It was his machinations that had almost thrown the election a few months before, and it was thanks to him and Hans Silver that random folk in town had been struck down with a sleeping curse.

Had *he* known the queen was coming to town? Was his plan to *do* something to her during the Harvest Festival?

"I just hope he waits until after the Harvest Festival," Bev said to Biscuit, her trusty laelaps, a magic-detecting creature that resembled a small, golden-furred dog. "I'd really like to win first place in the breadmaking contest."

With all the excitement of the sleeping curse, then Rustin's sacking, and now the queen's arrival, Bev's focus had been taken away from her true goal for the Harvest Festival. The year prior, she'd entered only after being strong-armed by Hendry and had surprised herself by winning second place. She'd spent the last year perfecting her recipe, adding in a longer proof in her root cellar to really let the flavors develop, and she wanted nothing more than to take home that first-place ribbon.

But as much as she'd hoped to avoid thinking about the queen, Andres, and the rest of it, she couldn't escape it. At dinner, her usual diners were aflutter with the news. The only one actually excited about it was Bardoff Boyd, the local schoolteacher, who'd studied in Queen's Capital and seemed to land on the side of all things not-magical. The rest of the diners—Earl Dollman, the local carpenter, Etheldra Dawes, the tea shop owner, and Max Sterling, the librarian—took the news with a grim sort of resignation.

"What do you reckon, Bev?" Etheldra asked. "What would the queen want with Pigsend?"

"Nothing good," Max muttered, earning a tsk from Bardoff.

"Oh, don't be glum! Her Majesty's always traveling the country, getting to know her subjects," Bardoff said. "There's nothing to be sad or worried about. We should be proud that she's decided to pay us a visit."

"Proud, yeah. Suspicious, more like. Maybe she got tired of hearing about all the mischief happening around town and is coming to oversee the stopping of it herself," Etheldra said.

"Well, would that be the worst thing?" Bardoff asked. "Bev, I'm sure you're tired of being dragged into every single thing that goes wrong around here."

"I'm not forming an opinion," Bev said. "I'd like to focus on my bread. Haven't had nearly the time to practice on it that I wanted."

"If the queen cancels the festival, there won't be a need to bake bread for it," Etheldra said with a look.

"How are you feeling?" Bev asked, deciding to force a subject change. "And Max? Any lingering effects from the curse?"

Both shook their heads. "Felt like I got the best sleep of my life," Etheldra said. "Haven't slept well since, but I doubt that's the curse's fault. We lost our apothecary."

"That's not true," Max said. "Stella's doing an admirable job."

Etheldra made a face. "Is she?"

Bev's focus went to her food as her face heated. The previous apothecary, Bernard, had been dabbling in magical tinctures where necessary. One such tincture had been requested by Etheldra for her and Earl's *honeymoon phase*. No wonder Etheldra was grumpy about Bernard's departure.

"Bernard was the one who poisoned you," Bardoff said.

"I'm not convinced of *that*," Etheldra said. "What did he have to gain from it? Why now?" She once again turned her hawklike eyes on Bev. "What do *you* think, Bev?"

"I think he fled," Bev said, hoping for a neutral face. "I think someone with a lot of magic helped him escape. Whether he's guilty or not..." She shrugged. "Too many unanswered questions."

In truth, Bernard had been the unfortunate patsy of Andres's plan to fire Rustin. Andres had gotten a recipe from Shamus, a wizard apprentice in Lower Pigsend. In return, Shamus came to save Bernard from being arrested, and presumably got him settled in Lower Pigsend as their apothecary, alongside Bernard's hapless brother Gerry. The other apothecary's skills had left a lot to be desired, and clearly the denizens of Lower Pigsend had been willing to do whatever it took to get a better apothecary.

The whole episode made Bev angry, especially as Andres insisted no harm had come to anyone. But Bernard was now essentially trapped underground, and his shop—his life's work—was in the hands of his assistant Stella Brewer. She couldn't imagine he was pleased about any of it.

"Hmph." Etheldra scrutinized Bev's face. "Fine. Keep your secrets. They all come out eventually."

The next day, it was midmorning when Bev finally saw Vellora in the butcher shop. Bev put aside her cleaning, which she wanted to get done before the Harvest Festival got underway, and hurried across the street, worried the butcher might disappear again. But Vellora had a bright smile when Bev walked in, as if she hadn't been affiliated with the group cursing people all over town.

"Morning, Bev. What's on the menu tonight?"

"Is Ida here?"

"She's out doing festival things," Vellora said with an affable smile. "Why?"

"Did Andres know the queen is coming?" Bev asked. "And is he planning to muck anything up? I'd like to know ahead of time, please, so I don't run off on another wild goose chase."

Vellora's face dropped. "Bev, we shouldn't talk about that—"

"I don't care," Bev said. "There's no one around, is there?"

The butcher let out a breath. "Andres doesn't tell me everything. He doesn't tell *anyone* everything. I swear on my wife's life, I had no idea he was behind the cursing."

"And now that you do, you still stand beside him?" Bev asked.

"Yes, because a small amount of pain now is worth the gain we'll have in the future," Vellora said. "My wife, never having to wake up in the middle of the night in fear because there's another soldier sleeping across the street. That's the world I want to live in."

"Did he know the queen is coming?" Bev reiterated. "And that Karolina was going to stick around and take over for Rustin?"

"I don't know," Vellora said emphatically. "I swear to you."

"Then what are your instructions from him?" Bev asked. "Surely, he's heard about the queen coming. Surely, he's heard about Karolina."

Vellora gestured to the shop. "Press on as if nothing's wrong. Support my wife in the Harvest Festival. Keep my head down. The usual."

Bev deflated. "That's it?"

"What? Did you expect him to try something?" Vellora asked. "Andres is a brilliant military strategist. He's going to strike when the situation warrants it. But he's not going to act impulsively." She smiled at Bev, a little bashfully. "For my part, I'm sorry you got roped into all that again. If I'd known he was behind it, I would've told you to stand down."

Bev appreciated that, but she couldn't help carrying a little anger. "I don't know why you're so loyal to him. He doesn't care about the people he's hurting. Bernard—"

"Bernard is fine," Vellora said.

"Are you sure?" Bev said. "Does he know why he was framed?"

"Well, no, but he's flourishing down in…well, down there." Vellora smiled. "He's got more business than he knows what to do with."

"I'm sure Gerry loves that," Bev muttered. "I

still don't think what Andres did was right."

"This is war, Bev—"

"No, it's not. It's Pigsend," Bev said. "And the sooner your lot figure that out, the better my life will be."

Chapter Two

The next two weeks passed in a flurry of activity. Bev couldn't believe all the small details that went into the Harvest Festival—and it kept her, Lillie, Ida, and even Hendry moving nonstop. There was still the inn to manage and dinner to serve on top of everything, as well as Bev's own preparations for hosting large crowds. But as things do, the time passed, the work got done, and finally the day before the Harvest Festival arrived.

Bev's job for the day was to manage the influx of vendors who'd be selling their wares in the town square under a sea of white tents. It was an eclectic mix of people: food merchants who fried up delicious, sweet fried dough and juicy turkey legs, artists and sculptors with amazing pieces for amazingly expensive prices, and the errant jewelry maker and woodworker. The year before, Hendry'd had the bright idea to have the local farmers sell in the midst of all the other vendors, keeping the crowds centered in town. It meant more tables, more people, and a bit more organizing, especially with the dragon fountain in the center again.

"Bloody awful thing," Alice Estrich grumbled as she held tight to the neighing and bucking horse attached to her wagon. "And why are there so many people here already?"

"Everyone's getting set up," Bev said, keeping a steady hand on the wagon. "C'mon, we're nearly there."

Alice managed to get her horse past the gigantic fountain, after which he calmed and allowed her to lead him down the narrow pathways to her spot.

"A bit far off from the middle of town, don't you think?" she said to Bev as she patted her horse on the nose. "Ida promised me I'd be front and center."

"I'd say center enough," Bev said, walking to the back of the wagon. "Let me help."

The wagon was overfull of produce, which Alice said was intentional. "I don't want to have to refill mid-week, you know? Hard enough getting here today."

"That's a good idea."

"Just hope no more magical nonsense happens," she said, grabbing a large crate of potatoes from the back. "Remember that stampede? Never did figure out how that happened."

"Magical nonsense," Bev said with a tight smile.

In reality, Claude Renault, a queen's soldier masquerading as a Harvest Festival judge, had cast a spell to send an imaginary herd of farm animals trampling through the vendor market. The creatures were made from magic, but the damage was real enough. His aim had been to clear out the town hall so he could test each of the Harvest Festival entries for traces of magic, and he'd almost succeeded.

"With the queen on her way, I doubt we'll see any tomfoolery from her people, in any case," Bev finished.

"The queen." Alice shivered. "What brought that about, d'ya know?"

"I hope someone will ask her when she gets here," Bev said evasively. "And in the meantime, we'll just continue on like normal."

"Hard to believe she'd find anything interesting about Pigsend," Alice said. "But in case she wants to stop by, I've made a couple extra pieces of jewelry."

She held up a woven necklace that looked more like a spiderweb than jewelry. Bev didn't know anything about fashion, so it could've been the latest and greatest thing, but it still looked rather unappealing to her.

"I'm sure she'll find it lovely," she managed after a beat. "And I hope you sell out of them. From what I can tell, it's going to be a big crowd. Lots of people coming to stay in Middleburg, and lots more finding spare rooms in Pigsend. It's going to be our biggest one ever, you know?"

"I'm sure folks are just eager to catch a glimpse of the queen," Alice said, pulling the last of her goods off the wagon. "Thanks for the help, Bev. Gonna get this put away then take Gus back home. We'll be sure to avoid the fountain this time."

Bev told her she was glad to help then spun on her heel and headed back into the crowd. Most everyone was working to set up their tables, and Bev didn't see many familiar faces amongst them. But that was usual for the festival. The vendors themselves traveled from place to place, and many of them had set their tents up east of town to sleep overnight.

"Watch where you're going!"

Bev turned, spotting Karolina Hunter berating a pair of vendors who were walking her way carrying a huge crate. It seemed to Bev that the queen's soldier should've moved, but Karolina had proven herself above offering even the littlest kindness to anyone in Pigsend, and stood her ground as the vendors maneuvered around her.

Bev hoped to avoid being seen, but winced as Karolina's voice rang out, "You! Innkeeper!"

"Yes, Ms. Hunter?" she said, forcing a smile. "What can I do for you?"

"Where is that confounded mayor?" she barked.

"I haven't a clue. Probably skittering about getting ready for the opening ceremonies tomorrow," Bev said. "Is there something I can help you with?"

"There are far too many people crammed into this square," she said, her cheeks rosy with anger. "There's no way Her Majesty is going to be able to get through."

Bev turned from side to side. There were at least four stride lengths between each row of booths.

"She has a *group* that walks *with her*," Karolina said, as if that sort of thing were obvious. "These booths need to be moved and spaced out more."

"I'm afraid that's quite impossible," Bev said. "Ida very carefully measured the square and the space, and we've got no more room than what's here."

Karolina's nostrils flared, but Bev held her gaze. She might be a queen's soldier, but in the few weeks she'd been serving as Pigsend's interim sheriff, Bev had learned she was quite a barker without much bite.

"The rules state—"

"Yes, we're well acquainted with that book now," Bev said. "As I said, Ida measured and ensured we were within the letter of the law. There's nothing we want more than this Harvest Festival to go off without a hitch, and that includes hosting Her Majesty and all her…requirements." Bev gestured to the booths on either side of her. "I suppose her group will just have to walk a step in front of her."

"No one walks in front of the queen."

"Then behind her. Whatever makes Her Majesty happy. But the space is the space, and while I'm sure Her Majesty is quite formidable, I don't think she can make more space out of nothing."

Especially considering the queen had outlawed and imprisoned people with such ability. But Bev kept that notion to herself.

~

Bev spent most of the day in the town square helping people get settled and getting things they needed, like twine, sandbags, and rags to clean their tables. But four o'clock arrived, and she had to bid farewell to the job of Harvest Festival co-chair and return to the real work at the Weary Dragon.

Dinner was bubbling away in the oven—Bev had assumed she'd be gone most of the afternoon, so she'd opted for a longer-cooking roast. The rosemary bread was ready to be put in beside it and would be brown and delicious in plenty of time for dinner. Bev had met lots of the vendors, many of whom hadn't known that dinner at the Weary Dragon was open to anyone with a silver coin, and they'd indicated they might be by for a hot meal.

Biscuit, who'd been keeping an eye on the inn all day, wagged his tail when Bev began peeling and chopping potatoes. She tossed him a few skins, smiling as he gobbled them up, and tutted.

"You know, it strikes me that you've been living at the inn a whole year, Mr. Biscuit," she said.

He was too busy sniffing the ground for any morsel that might've been left behind to pay attention.

It had been ages since she'd considered where he'd actually come from. He'd appeared on her compost pile then made himself at home at the inn. She'd searched high and low for his owner, but he'd seemed to like his new home, and she found him useful, so she didn't press the subject.

But some part of her wondered if his owner would finally come to claim him. It made her awfully sad to think about, so she didn't dwell on it.

"We'll cross that bridge when we come to it," she said, tossing him another skin. "Let's just hope the opening day of the festival goes smoothly."

The dining room was full when she brought out dinner, and she was a bit concerned she might not have enough. Etheldra, of course, was right up front, and filled her plate higher than normal, as if proving a point. The rest of the diners took a smaller portion, and in the end, there was plenty to go around. Even Biscuit got a little bit of gristle.

The conversations were loud, and Bev rather

enjoyed the energy in the room. So many nights it was just the usual diners and whatever guests were passing through. Soon, when the weather got colder, it would be even quieter, with guests dwindling until the only ones coming to eat were locals. The festival always felt like a last hurrah before everything went to sleep for the winter.

Midway through the meal, Rustin slumped inside. Since losing his job, he'd been more aimless and depressed, but at least he'd been coming to dinner at the Weary Dragon for some company. Bev hadn't had the heart to charge him, especially as his current state of joblessness was due to external factors.

"All gone?" he asked morosely as he came up to the table of food.

"I saved you a plate," Bev said, running to grab it from the back. "Wasn't sure you were going to make it."

"I meant to be here on time, but Karolina had me off on some errands again." He gestured to his muddy boots. "I had to ensure there weren't any tall plants in Grant's field where Her Majesty's going to 'be setting up camp. Spent all day stomping them down."

Bev cleared her throat lightly. "I think Grant Klose has a goat or two. You could've enlisted him to help."

Rustin's eyes widened, then he let out a loud

sigh. "You know, maybe Karolina's right. I'm too dumb to do anything but look pretty." His shoulders drooped. "I spent all day out there, too. And she didn't even say thank you."

"Thank you, Rustin, for all you're doing," Bev said. "But you know…you don't work for Karolina anymore. If anything, you're a volunteer for the Harvest Festival. You're allowed to tell her no, if you want."

"I know, I know, but…" He lifted a shoulder. "I thought maybe if I did a good job, a *real* good job, Her Majesty might order me back to my job, you know? Maybe if she saw how much I did for everyone, she might change her mind about me." He shook his head. "But if it's up to Karolina, that won't happen. She just hates me for no reason."

"I think she feels that way about everyone in Pigsend," Bev muttered. "Don't let it get to you, Rustin. One more week, then hopefully she'll be moving on to terrorize some other town."

"Are you talking about Ms. Hunter?" Bardoff said, coming up to stand next to Rustin. "Have you heard when Her Majesty's supposed to arrive?"

"She doesn't tell me anything," Rustin said. "Except to yell at me."

"Go have a seat, Rustin," Bev said. "Eat up. It's going to be a long day tomorrow."

Rustin left her and Bardoff, who seemed barely able to contain his excitement. "I do hope she arrives tomorrow. I've been preparing the children for her."

"Oh? How so?"

"Well, I've got a quartet of decent singers," he said. "They'll sing her official song. I plan on opening with that. Then I'm having a few read some of the epic poems written about her. The children have been rehearsing them all week. I'd like them to be recited from memory, just to be able to show Her Majesty how loyal her subjects are out here."

Bev smiled. "I'm sure the children are as excited as you are."

"They don't care, actually," Bardoff admitted. "I think many of them… Well, they were too young to remember the war. And I've gotten one or two nasty notes from parents who've pulled their children from class after they came home with the poetry memorization lesson."

Bev wasn't surprised. "I see."

"But still. She's *our* queen. We should show her some respect. That's how I was raised, and that's how I expect the children to behave." He puffed out his chest. "So… If you happen to hear when she's arriving, I'd love to be there to greet her."

"You'll be the first person I tell," Bev said with a smile.

He gave her his plate and beamed. "I hear she's staying in her own campsite to the south of here. But I hope if she does come to town, she's able to taste your amazing rosemary bread. You are entering it in the contest this year, aren't you?"

"I'm planning on it," Bev said. She already had her ingredients set aside to make the dough this evening. And she was planning on asking Biscuit to sleep in the kitchen to keep an eye on it. "Have a good night, Bardoff. We'll see you in the morning."

As soon as he was gone, Max took his place. "I've been hearing the children rehearse for two weeks now. It's awful."

Bev barked a laugh. "Oh, Max. I'm sure it's not all that bad."

"Ballads and stanzas about her bravery and strength." He made a disgusted face. "Not to mention, I don't think Bardoff knows how to carry a tune, so the children are horribly off-key. I've taken to putting cotton in my ears just so I can think."

"I take it you're going to make yourself scarce?" Bev asked.

"I will be at my post," Max said with a sniff as he pulled on his cloak. "If Her Majesty is interested in reading about the history of Pigsend, I'm happy to serve her, as I serve everyone who comes through my door. But I won't like it."

Etheldra and Earl weren't far behind him, as Etheldra declared she needed to test another round of pies before her contest in two days. Earl winced, declaring he couldn't possibly eat another slice, but quickly silenced himself after a glare from his wife.

Then it was just the vendors, who seemed nice enough, and who were grateful to sit indoors with a hot meal they didn't have to cook themselves.

"So you just travel the country in tents?" Bev asked one, who called himself Reginald. "It must be a lonely life."

"We travel in packs sometimes," he said, gesturing to the folks at his table. "It's a small community, but there are so many festivals, often we have to divide and conquer. I haven't seen Allister over there since the spring, but Johnny and I traveled in from Cirsatown just last night. The first few days, we all get together and figure out who's been where and how they did."

"I see." Bev nodded. "And what do you sell?"

"I'm a woodworker, myself. Allister sells fried dough. Johnny makes windchimes."

Bev couldn't see an industry for that but nodded just the same. "Well, we're glad to have you in Pigsend for the festival. The vendors certainly make it much more appealing for those who come into town."

"Erm, we heard a rumor that Her Majesty is going to be here," Reginald said. "Is that true?"

"As far as I'm aware, yes," Bev said. "But as to the specifics, I haven't a clue."

"That'll be something, eh, boys?" Reginald said to his compatriots. "Never seen royalty before."

"So…" Bev tilted her head. "The queen's never showed up at any festival before?"

"Nope. This is a once-in-a-lifetime opportunity for us," he said with a grin. "Can't wait to shake her hand!"

Bev doubted that these vendors, as lovely as they were, would be allowed to get close to Her Majesty. But despite all her reservations, Bev found herself a little excited, too. She'd never seen royalty before, either (at least, to her memory), and she hoped the queen found Pigsend as delightful as Bev did.

Chapter Three

Bev couldn't help but feel the jitters as the first day of the Harvest Festival dawned. The opening ceremonies would begin around ten-thirty, and later this afternoon, Bev would be bringing one of the six loaves she had proofing to the breadmaking contest (the others, of course, would be served at dinner).

Her very first stop this morning was her root cellar, where three loaves of perfectly-risen bread dough were waiting. She exhaled a sigh of relief. Last year's perfectly-risen loaf had disappeared off her table (again, thanks to Claude). There were still hours to go before the first judging, though, so Bev didn't feel she'd relax until the slice was on a plate and headed for a judge's mouth.

Speaking of the judges, if history was any indication, they'd be arriving this morning before the contests began. The first judge, Alice Winter, had been judging the Pigsend Harvest Festival for over two decades, and Bev was overjoyed to hear she was resuming her position after being put off the year before by Claude. The other judge was Mr. Piers Warford, and he'd come with a long list of accomplishments declaring him a senior member of the Queen's judging corps.

The rest of the inn was fully booked with regular returning contestants and visitors. Ira Bower, a sweet old man who'd entered the knitting contest every year and never once won as much as a runner-up spot, was scheduled to come, as was Mandisa Munson, who'd won second place in the jam-making contest last year. Carl Flogger and his husband Dwain were also in town for the fiber arts contest, as Carl had lots of crocheted pieces. Isolde Prince and her husband Harold had come to stay for the first time, snagging the room Bev had opened up when she'd decided to room the two judges together. Isolde was entering the jam contests, too, though she'd gone home without an award the year before. Lastly, Gena Hann, who used to live in town before moving to Sheepsburg, was in town just to enjoy the festivities.

Mr. Warford was the first to arrive, walking through the door promptly at nine in the morning.

He had a severe look about him, with black hair and pale skin, and lips that seemed to have never seen a smile. Bev hadn't thought *anyone* could be more intense than Petula Banks, but Warford seemed to edge her out.

"We're glad to have you," Bev told him as she retrieved his key. "I do hope it's all right, but we've got a full house this evening, and I've got you staying with the other judge, Ms. Winter."

"Yes, that's quite all right. I'm used to it with these smaller towns." He looked around, and based on his expression, seemed to find the Weary Dragon acceptable. "I've been in touch with my former colleague Petula Banks."

"Ah, yes. Ms. Banks has been through a couple times now," Bev said. "She's been promoted to election monitor."

"Indeed, she has. We were sorry to lose her, but I understand she was destined for greater things." He adjusted his glasses on his nose. "But she did tell me all about the mishaps that happened last festival. I do hope we won't have any of the same this year. I must warn you, I'm not one for tomfoolery."

"Neither am I," Bev said. "Especially with Her Majesty coming to town. We're all going to be on our best behavior."

He nodded approvingly. "Petula spoke very highly of you, Ms. Bev. She said you were someone I could trust if things went sideways. I do appreciate having such a person in a town like this."

"I'm also on the festival planning committee, so whatever you need, I'm happy to provide," Bev said, pleased Petula had been so kind. "If you'd like, once the rest of the guests arrive, I can take you on a tour of town."

"That would be lovely."

"Here." Bev picked up a basket of muffins beside her. "Have a muffin to tide you over."

He held up his hands. "I mustn't be swayed by any sort of sweet, Ms. Bev. It's imperative I remain neutral as I judge each contest."

Bev cracked a smile. "They were made by the bakers next door, neither of whom are entering any contest. And they're complimentary with the room. But if you'd rather not..."

"On second thought..." He snatched one from the basket. "I'm quite famished."

"Help yourself to as many as you like," Bev said. "But...if you're worried about impropriety, then you might want to avoid the rosemary bread I'll be serving with dinner. I'm entering it into the breadmaking contest."

"Hm." He nodded slowly. "I appreciate the heads-up."

Bev showed him to his room and helped him get settled then returned just as another set of guests were coming in—Ira Bower and Ms. Winter. Poor Ms. Winter looked quite frail, as if the journey from

Middleburg had taken nearly everything out of her. Ira, no spring chicken himself, was helping her into the inn and settled her on one of the chairs.

"Glad to see you both," Bev said. "It's going to be a wonderful festival. Alice, we did miss you last year."

She smiled. "Glad to be back. Though I have to say, I think this is my last year. Getting up there in age, you know." She patted Ira weakly on the arm. "Can't keep up with these young bucks!"

"Oh, you." Ira chuckled. "Good to see you again, Bev. The town looks great! As does the inn."

"I've certainly been scrubbing it," Bev said. "Are you feeling good about your chances this year, Ira?"

He sighed. "I always hope it's my year. Maybe this year I'll just hope otherwise and be pleasantly surprised. Kinda looking forward to seeing Her Majesty." He looked around. "She's, erm, not staying here, is she?"

"No, no. She's got her own setup to the south of here," Bev said. "Oh, Ms. Winter, did you get my note about rooming with the other judge?"

"I did." She nodded. "As long as he doesn't mind my snoring, I think we'll be just fine."

"And if he does, I'm happy to share my room," Ira said.

Bev actually thought Warford *might* care, but she was optimistic she wouldn't have to move anyone. "Let's hope that's not the case. Mr. Warford seems mostly pleasant, in any case. I'm taking him on a tour around town before the festival opens, if anyone would like to join us.""

"Oh, goodness me, I don't think I can do that," Alice said. "It'll be all I can do to get to the bread judging this evening. I'm going to go upstairs and have a nap, if that's all right?"

Bev certainly didn't have a problem with that, and as soon as she got Alice in her room, the front door opened again and the rest of her guests streamed in. Bev welcomed them all and helped get their luggage up the stairs. Then she asked if they'd like to join Mr. Warford on a tour, but they each declined, as they'd been to Pigsend many times over the years.

"I do wonder where the queen is staying," Mandisa said. "If only so I can avoid that area."

"And why would you want to avoid Her Majesty?" Warford asked with a suspicious glare.

"Not her, per se, but her people," she said, backtracking a little. "I'm sure they won't want villagers traipsing about their campsite."

"She's not arrived yet, as I understand it," Bev said. "But she'll be staying in the south, I believe."

"Good to know, erm… I think I'll head out for a stroll anyway. But in the opposite direction."

Warford kept his gaze on her all the way to the door then turned to Bev. "I've got very little patience for people who don't have respect for our queen. I do hope this town isn't full of people with that opinion."

"I think you'll find Pigsend lovely," Bev said, trying to be evasive. "And ready to welcome the queen whenever she arrives."

They left the inn after that, with Bev pointing out the bakery next door and the butcher shop. She was grateful Warford didn't want to stop in either, because if he was looking for someone who disliked the queen, he'd find it in Vellora and Hans Silver. The farmer had volunteered to spend the week helping Vellora while Ida flitted around with the Harvest Festival, but Bev had to wonder if there was an ulterior motive, too. She still couldn't look Hans in the eye after what he'd done to the citizens of Pigsend.

"Pardon, Ms. Bev, were you going to keep telling me about the town?" Warford asked.

"Yes, sorry," Bev said, realizing she'd been staring into the butcher shop. "The town square is just up this way. We've put all the vendors there. It's a nice mix of local farmers and traveling folk." She glanced at him, remembering the squabble with Karolina earlier. "We've made sure to follow the regulations on the distance between booths. Ida Witzel—she's our chair—made sure of that."

"I've been in communication with Ms. Witzel," he said with a nod. "She seems quite adept at managing this festival. What is her trade?"

"She's a butcher," Bev said. "Her family's been in town for decades." She turned back toward the upcoming square. "We've just recently reinstalled our dragon fountain. You'll see it above all the tents. We have a sculptor who lives in town—Ramone Comely. They were able to get everything fixed back up after the fountain was destroyed last year."

"I heard about that," he said. "A sinkhole, wasn't it? I hope they aren't common here."

Not unless Karolina's stopping the magical river. "It's been a year since. I think it was just a curious circumstance. We've had a few of those over the past year."

"Mm."

They stepped into the vendor space, immediately bathed in the sounds and smells of activity. The festival hadn't officially opened yet, but already there were throngs of people milling about.

"You're sure this is regulation?" Warford asked, looking at the space between the booths. "Four stride lengths?"

Bev nodded, realizing perhaps too late that they should've used tall Vellora's stride instead of her petite wife's. "Ida would be happy to show you."

"No need." Warford pulled a small leather-bound notebook out of his pocket and made a notation. "And where will the rest of the contests be held?"

Bev gave him the rundown, explaining that the

town hall would be used for most of the judging contests, including food and fiber arts. The livestock judging would be north of town. And the vendors were right in the town square.

"Everything is centralized," Bev said. "Today we have the opening ceremonies, and we'll have the first round of the breadmaking contest."

"Which you'll be entering," he said.

"Ida assures me that as long as I have no involvement with the judges, it's perfectly legal," Bev said.

"Except you're housing me and giving me a tour. That might raise some eyebrows."

Bev stopped and turned to him. "If this is a problem, I'm happy to leave you to your own wandering. The mayor paid for your bed and meals out of the town's funds. I'm just cooking the food and cleaning the sheets."

He surveyed her then, to her immense relief, shook his head. "No, that won't be necessary. I just wanted to make sure you knew the rules."

"Backward and forward," Bev said. Even if she hadn't been keen on entering the breadmaking contest, she still would've had the whole lot memorized with how often she'd referred to them with the planning committee. "As I said, we're eager to run a festival without any mishaps."

"There will *always* be mishaps," he said, pausing to sniff Allister's fried dough stand. "You, sir. I take it you have a license to sell that food?"

"O'course I do," Allister said, retrieving a small handwritten and stamped paper. "Pay my fifty gold coins every year to Her Majesty for the privilege."

"Fifty gold coins!" Bev couldn't help but exclaim. "To sell fried dough?"

"A very important piece of paper," Warford said. "Otherwise, we'll have anyone trying to sell anything. Her Majesty is keen on order and structure. Every single industry under the sun has requirements—"

"Not mine," Bev said. "At least, not that I know of."

"I'm sure the rulebook for innkeeping is coming," he said with a haughty sniff. "An inn must be run with standards of cleanliness and professionalism."

"I think you'll find the Weary Dragon is known for that already," Bev said. "But, should Her Majesty send me a book of how to run my inn, I'll be sure to adhere to it in any ways I'm not currently."

That seemed to satisfy him, but only until the next booth, where he questioned Johnny's windchimes, and his license to sell "miscellaneous decor." To Bev's surprise, Johnny also had a license for that, as did Reginald for selling his woodworking, and the next vendor for selling jewelry.

"Oh, no," Bev muttered as they turned the

corner to the farmers' market section and she spotted Alice and her jewelry. "Erm, I think it's about time for the opening ceremony."

"No, it's not. It's not ten-thirty," he said. "Besides that, I think I see something I'd like to question."

He marched right up to Alice, whose face brightened into a wide smile as she had no idea what was coming. "Good morning! Can I interest you in—"

"Do you have a license for selling fruits and vegetables?" he asked. "And this…whatever this is."

"It's jewelry," she said, shifting uncomfortably as she looked at Bev for help. "And, um. No. No, I don't."

He actually looked happy. "Well, I regret to inform you that *every* vendor in the marketplace is *required* to have a license and pay a fee. The total for selling fruits and vegetables is fifty gold coins, paid annually."

"I'm sorry, *what?*" Alice jumped to her feet. "Bev, what in the world is this? I've been selling at the farmers' market for ages and never had to pay a single coin."

Warford turned to Bev. "Is that so? An illegal farmers' market?"

"I don't know about illegal," Bev said. "And this is the farmers' market section. They're not…"

Well, she didn't know if they were required to

have a license or not. Ida had handled most of the registrations.

"I don't have that kind of money," Alice said, her voice shaky.

"Then I'm afraid I have no choice but to tell you to pack up your things and leave." He adjusted his tunic. "I will be back within the hour. If you aren't gone, I will have to fetch security."

"Now, wait just a minute," Bev said.

"I will not wait a minute. The rules and regulations are here for a *reason*." He sniffed at her. "Her Majesty would be horrified if she found out there were unlicensed vendors here."

"The entire row is unlicensed," Bev said, gesturing to the farmers. "Because they've never had to have one—"

"But that's what you don't understand. It's been mandatory for two years. And I'm afraid I have no choice but to report this illegal market up the chain." He looked around, seemingly energized by this new mission. "Until all vendors are properly licensed and accounted for, this and any other farmers' market will be closed."

"What do you mean, any other market?" Bev said. "You mean they aren't allowed to sell at the Harvest Festival, right? There's a biweekly one outside of town, but surely—"

"It, too, will be shut down until further notice." He lifted his chin. "Now, Ms. Bev, I must continue my inspection. Especially as it seems this festival is not quite as well-run as it would seem."

Chapter Four

Warford wasn't even five steps away before Alice burst into tears. Bev hurried to her side, comforting her with a pat on the shoulder while glaring at the judge's retreating back.

"W-what a-am I g-gonna do?" she stammered. "The farmers' market? Gone? How am I gonna sell my wares? I-I c-can't p-pay my b-bills if I c-can't sell my p-produce!"

"Don't you worry," Bev said. "I'm going to find Hendry and have a word with her about it. I'm sure there's something in the rulebook...some kind of clause."

But as Bev found Hendry, it seemed the news had already reached the mayor, who wore a grim look of resignation. "It seems we were *remiss* in using last year's festival regulations book, as it had been updated with some key new information that's put us on the back foot. I have no choice but to ask the farmers' market to pack up their things and leave—unless they're willing to pay the fee."

"Warford said there were to be no more farmers' markets," Bev said. "Even the biweekly one."

"And he's well within his rights to do that," Hendry said, though it seemed the idea left a foul taste in her mouth. "Per the laws, the Pigsend farmers' market *technically* falls under festivals, even though it's held every week. If he wants to shut it down permanently, he can."

"Fifty gold coins to the queen just to sell a crate of carrots," Bev said. "That's outrageous. Why didn't Petula say anything about it last year?"

"Because, as I said, it's a new regulation, and we prepared for the festival using last year's manual. Apparently, the queen likes to update things on a regular basis." Hendry adjusted her tunic with pursed lips. "I don't like it any more than you do, Bev, but my hands are tied. Warford seems inclined to find something wrong with this festival. Maybe he works for Miranda..."

"Don't start that again," Bev muttered. "We've not heard anything from the Middleburg folks in weeks. Let's keep it that way."

"Wilda's still entering the pie-making contest,"

Hendry said with a look. "But in any case, Mr. Warford wants the farmers gone as soon as possible, so I'll leave you to handle that."

"I've got to get back to the inn to tend to my bread and get dinner going," Bev said before snapping her fingers. "Sounds like a good job for Rustin. That'll keep him busy today."

"Good. Go find him," Hendry said, turning on her heel and walking away.

~

But Rustin wasn't anywhere to be found. Bev searched his house, the sheriff's office, and even asked some of the vendors if they'd seen him. By the time she returned to the farmers' market section to take care of it herself, she found it empty—and Karolina Hunter directing some of the remaining vendors to move their booths.

"What's going on?" Bev asked, rushing over. "The farmers cleared out?"

"Indeed. Now we can space things out as they're supposed to be," Karolina said, keeping her gaze on the vendors. "When Her Majesty gets here, this will be much more to her liking."

Bev scowled, irked by all the changes that were happening to the festival already, but swallowed her anger. "Have you seen Rustin?"

"Why would I keep track of that dolt?" she snapped. "No, no. Over *here*, you moron. Right here." She stormed away, all but yanking a table out of the hands of two vendors to put it in the right spot.

The town hall clock chimed, and Bev winced. She'd wasted an hour searching for Rustin, and now she'd have to rush through getting dinner ready if she wanted it to cook while she was at the breadmaking contest. She hated leaving the vendors to Karolina's oversight, but she really didn't have a choice.

She spun on her heel and rushed back to the inn, but didn't find her meat where it was supposed to be. Bev assumed that, like her, Ida had been waylaid by something or another. So, she stoked the oven to get it hot then headed across the street.

Unfortunately, Hans was there, and Vellora was nowhere to be seen. Bev forced herself to be nice as she stepped inside.

"It seems my meat delivery was forgotten," Bev said, keeping her distance. "Is it ready?"

"Oh, right!" Hans gave her a bright smile. "Let me go get it for you. Sorry, still trying to get the hang of everything." He beckoned her to follow him into the back. "How's the festival going? I've seen so many people walk by the shop. We don't get to see much from our house, so it's a nice treat to be so close. I told Fred we should think about taking a turn around the market, once Vellora's back from her deliveries."

"Is that where she is?" Bev asked. "Delivering

meat?"

"What else would she be doing?" Hans asked with a chuckle.

"Meeting with Andres? Preparing for the queen's arrival?"

Hans almost tripped, looking at Bev with something akin to guilt. "We've got our orders."

"And they are?"

"Heads down, act like normal," he said.

"Is that before or after you curse more people?" Bev really shouldn't have mentioned it, but she couldn't believe Hans was acting like his part in the escapade was no big deal.

He wilted. "I'm sorry we didn't tell you."

"Don't apologize to me. Apologize to Trent, Herman, Max, Etheldra, and Eldred." Bev crossed her arms. "And Bernard."

"Bernard is fine," Hans said. "And the rest are as well. Just had a nice nap, you know?"

Bev scowled, but didn't feel like arguing further. If Hans didn't see that what he'd done was wrong, Bev wasn't going to waste her precious time arguing with him.

"My meat, if you please."

~

Dinner went in the oven, as did six loaves of bread. Bev hovered over it, watching the clock with more than her usual amount of angst. She couldn't sit still, so she mopped the floor, deep cleaned the table, and ran a washrag over her canisters. Everything was, of course, already clean, but Bev needed the distraction.

Of course, she needn't have worried. She'd made rosemary bread almost every day for the past six years and knew the process backward and forward. When she pulled the tins from the oven, they were as perfect as any she served on a regular day. Whether they were *award-winning*, she didn't know, but the effort was done.

With the bread cooling, Bev finally sat on her kitchen stool and relaxed. Biscuit put his paws on her legs, and she patted him on the head.

"Well, all we can do, eh, Biscuit?" Bev said with a smile. "You know, maybe ol' Wim McKee was right about not entering the contest. It does cause all manner of stress. Might be happier if I didn't have to worry about it, you know?"

Biscuit ruffed.

"You're right. It was nice to win second last year," Bev said.

As the clock struck three, Bev tucked the prettiest loaf into a basket with a tea towel, along with her sharpest knife. Last year, she'd thought Staunton Bucko odd for bringing his own knife to cut his bread, but perhaps he was on to something. Or perhaps she was now just as odd as Mr. Bucko.

"Suppose we'll be seeing him again, hm, Biscuit?" Bev said with a sigh. "Let's put on our nicest face."

Biscuit walked beside her as they headed toward the town hall. The square, it seemed, held far fewer vendors than she'd seen earlier in the day—but perhaps that was just because everyone was more spread out. Bev just hoped Warford's rampage would end today, and things would be better tomorrow.

Unfortunately, when Bev got inside the town hall, the storm cloud followed. There were twenty entrants for the breadmaking contest, and each of them held their loaves as they scowled at Warford. The judge was inspecting Staunton's beautiful rye loaf roughly, pressing down on the crust without much care for the interior.

Ida handed Bev a number, twenty, and made a face that told Bev that her assessment of the situation was correct. Bev scanned the room, looking for Alice, and frowned when she didn't see her.

"Where is Ms. Winter?" Bev asked.

"I've dismissed her," Warford said, before Ida could speak.

"What do you mean, dismissed her?" Bev asked, stepping back in surprise. "She's been a Pigsend judge for decades."

"And it shows. She lacks the correct palette to adequately judge anything. I was anticipating such a thing would happen, so I've already sent for the alternate judge waiting in Middleburg."

"Alternate…" Bev sputtered. "What—"

"And I regret to inform you that we will be needing separate accommodations," he said. "I trust you will figure something out."

Before Bev could answer him, Warford turned back to Staunton. "Where did you source the flour for this rye?"

"What does it matter?" Staunton said, his cheeks darkening. "It's rye bread. It's won the last few years."

"Yes, well, it's a new year," Warford said. "And Her Majesty wants to ensure that everything is done correctly."

"What could possibly be incorrect about flour?" Bev asked.

Warford thrust the rye back into Staunton's hands and crossed the room, grabbing Bev's loaf and squeezing it so hard the crust cracked. "Well, in preparation for today's judging, I went to see the local flour mill to ensure everything was up to Her Majesty's standards. Unfortunately, he lacks the proper certifications to be running a mill of that size, so the mill has been closed until such time as he completes all the requisite licensures."

Bev couldn't believe what she was hearing. "What do you mean closed? Sonny's been operating that mill for thirty years!"

"And Her Majesty wants to make sure that

operation is fully in compliance with her highest standards of grain milling." Warford's smile was anything but kind. "And what's to say he hasn't been serving you barley when you'd asked for rye?"

Bev was quite sure Sonny knew the difference between grains. "Everyone here gets their flour from Sonny Gray. In fact, everyone between here and Middleburg gets their flour from him. If he's no longer in business, no one will be able to get flour or oats or anything else they need to make bread and feed themselves."

"Then I suggest you encourage Mr. Gray to complete his licensure," Warford said. "Because otherwise, I may have to consider canceling the breadmaking contest. Perhaps the pie-making one, too, if *everyone* gets their flour from him."

Ida shot a worried look at Bev, as did everyone else in the room, and Bev cleared her throat. "If you're worried about the quality, if everything was made with the same flour source, then the only deviation would be from the skill of the baker, right?"

He actually seemed to consider what she'd said. "I suppose…"

"So I think it's fine to continue the contest," Bev said. "If that's what we're worried about."

It seemed everyone held their breath as Warford mulled it over. Finally, with a heaving sigh, he nodded.

"Very well. But that miller will *have* to update his certifications in the coming days, else I will cancel these contests."

~

With one crisis averted, the breadmaking contestants offered their slices to Warford, who of course was going to judge by himself. He disappeared into the main office with Ida carrying the plates with him, and once the door was closed, everyone exhaled.

"That was close," Staunton said. "What climbed up his wheat stalk?"

"I haven't a clue," Bev said. She told him and the others about Warford shutting down the farmers' market, which earned a few surprised gasps from the group.

"He's off his rocker," Felicia Dinwight said, though she kept her voice quiet, so it wouldn't carry. "And closing Sonny's mill? What in the world? We'll be without flour in days."

"I've heard of this, actually," Staunton said, puffing out his chest. "Rumors and such have come to Middleburg. Her Majesty has exhausted all the money out of the former kingside country, and she's moving her insatiable appetite for gold to the more rural areas."

"What do you mean?" Bev asked.

"Well, it's all these *certifications* and *licenses*," Staunton said. "Pay up or you're outta luck. It's just a way to line the queen's coffers. What does she need fifty gold coins from a farmers' market vendor in Pigsend for? What could that possibly pay for other than her own jewels?"

Bev couldn't help but agree. "These queenside folks are often a bit too strict when they arrive. Maybe he'll lighten up as the festival wears on."

Petula certainly had, and when she'd come for the election, she'd loosened up even more. If only Bev could find some scandalous history about Warford, she'd be able to keep him from shutting down everything in town.

"I'm sure he's just concerned about Her Majesty coming here," said a bread maker whose name Bev didn't know, a little sheepishly. "A lot of pressure to be the judge in a festival. What if Her Majesty disagrees with his decision on which is the best bread?"

"Maybe Her Majesty's going to be tasting our bread," another bread maker, Boris Pearlman, said, a little excitedly.

Staunton sniffed loudly, as if the idea were abhorrent to him. "I doubt she's even going to show up. Seems like something she'd do. Make us all worry and fret over setting up the festival to suit her needs then never arrive."

That didn't seem the worst outcome to Bev, but all conversation ceased when Warford returned with a sheet of paper.

"I'm here to announce who will be moving on. Now, I want to be *clear* that if I should decide the lack of certification for the flour miller is a problem, I may just cancel the contest altogether. So if anyone wants to drop out, they're welcome to do so."

No one seemed to want to, so Warford cleared his throat.

"Breads number four, fifteen, seven, nineteen, and twenty. You are all on to the next stage."

Bev's heart slowed as the first four numbers called out weren't hers, but she grinned brightly when he called the last one. The farmers' market and Sonny's mill crises aside, she couldn't have been happier to be past the first stage.

"Now, as you recall, the final judging will take place in five days' time. Contestants are not required to submit the same recipe, and, in fact, I would encourage variety, especially with those using herbs not to my liking. Some of your bread squeaked by based on the texture and crumb alone. But if you want to win, taste will have to be taken into consideration."

Bev blinked. He couldn't possibly mean her rosemary bread, could he?

"Now, if you'll excuse me, I've got to continue my inspection of the vendor space."

He bustled out of the town hall, leaving the group in silence. Even the others who'd passed— which, unsurprisingly, included Staunton—had their excitement muted.

"Suppose I'll see you lot in four days," he said. "Long walk back to Middleburg, so I'd better get on it." He smiled at Bev, and she was surprised to find it genuine. "Happy you made it through. Though what was that about herbs, eh? I think you're the only one who uses them."

"Yes," Bev said. The rosemary was what made her bread delicious, but what happened when the judge wasn't a fan of it at all? She'd have to think about what to do. "In any case, I'd better get back to the inn and check on dinner. The rest of the town loves my bread, so…"

But as Bev left the town hall, intending to do just that, she ran almost headfirst into Mayor Hendry, who was looking concerned and worried—a rare sight for the positive and always-put-together mayor.

"What's wrong?" Bev asked.

"Were you able to find Rustin?" she asked, tapping her chin nervously.

Bev shook her head. "Karolina took over moving the farmers, and I had to get back to the inn. But they're all gone, so—"

"I'm not worried about the farmers," Hendry said. "I think… I think something's happened to him."

Chapter Five

"What do you mean, something's happened to him?" Bev said. "I'm sure he's running around somewhere. Or, more likely, lying low so Karolina won't yell at him again."

"He's not at his house. He's not in his office. No one at the festival's seen him all day," Hendry said, tapping her fingers off. "And his house… Bev, it looks like someone took him."

If it had been anyone else raising concern, Bev would've told them not to worry, that Rustin was fine, and he'd probably resurface after the festival. But Hendry wasn't the sort to get bent out of shape over anything.

"What do you want me to do?"

"Maybe you could see if your...erm...special dog could go looking for him?" Hendry asked. "You said he's got a good nose?"

Bev nodded. "He'd be happy to. C'mon, he's back at the inn, we can—"

"Oh, heavens, no." The old Hendry quickly snapped back into place. "I've got to stay amongst the people. You handle it, Bev dear. I'm sure your Cookie will find him right away, and all will be well."

"Biscuit," Bev corrected, shaking her head as Hendry walked away. She might've acted like she didn't care, but Bev had seen the worry in her eyes. And her dislike for the laelaps was well known, so she must've had to swallow a lot of pride to ask him for help.

Bev found said laelaps wagging his tail in front of the oven, ready for his part in the meal. Bev knelt and patted him on the head.

"Got a job for you, if you're up for it," Bev said. "Mayor Hendry thinks Rustin might be missing. Do you think you could sniff around town looking for him?"

Biscuit let out a ruff.

"I'll head over in the morning to check on his house," Bev said. "And don't worry, I'll save you a spot of dinner."

The laelaps scampered toward the open kitchen door, his nose pressed to the ground. Bev tried to assure herself that Rustin was *probably* fine, that he'd perhaps taken the chance of a busy town and Karolina preparing for the queen's arrival to disappear. She hoped he'd decided to make a new start somewhere else, and they'd get a nice letter from him in a few months detailing all he'd done.

But an unnerved part of her gut told her otherwise. The same part of her that knew Rustin had been the unfortunate target of Andres Rade's yet-to-be-revealed mission. He'd orchestrated an entire fiasco of curses and potions just to get Rustin fired. Or, more correctly, to ensure the sheriff position was vacant.

Semantics were, as it turned out, very important to Andres. Bev had mistakenly believed Andres had no information about her past when she'd first met him. But, at the time, he'd told her he had *nothing to share*. Which, as it turned out, didn't mean he didn't *have* information, just nothing he wanted to *share*. Ridiculous, but Bev knew now she needed to take him exactly at his word.

She pondered Rustin's disappearance and Andres's machinations as she finished up dinner. With the loaves of bread she'd baked with her contest entry sliced and placed in her basket, there would be more than enough for everyone.

But when she brought out the first plates of food, she frowned. There were, perhaps, half the usual number of people milling about—enough chairs for everyone, which was a rarity during the Harvest Festival. And there wasn't a smile among them.

"Dinner is, erm, served," Bev said.

Unsurprisingly, Etheldra was the first in line. "Looks like someone died, doesn't it?"

"Did someone die?" Bev asked, a little cautiously.

"From what I hear, people are getting shut down by that judge of yours," Etheldra said, scooping more than her usual portion onto her plate. "About half the vendors didn't have the right whatever, so they were told to pack it in and leave."

"And what's this I hear about the farmers' market being permanently closed?" Earl asked. "For what reason?"

"The queen's rules, I guess," Max said, behind Earl. "Outrageous what they're doing. There's no need to pay all that gold just to open shop."

"Her Majesty is doing what she thinks is best," Bardoff said.

His words of affirmation toward the queen silenced the chatter in the room.

"Is she now?" Etheldra asked. "Or is she just trying to line her pockets?"

"It's all for our protection," Bardoff said. "In Queen's Capital, I had to retake all my certifications to be able to teach the kids. She wants to ensure every industry has the most qualified individuals."

"Why does she want fifty gold coins from us, then?" one of the vendors barked.

"To pay all the people harassing the vendors, of course," Etheldra said. "Is that confounded woman here yet? Thought she was coming to the Harvest Festival. Suppose a queen can be late."

"Her name is Queen Meandra," Bardoff said, his cheeks turning red. "Or Her Majesty."

"When she comes, I'll be sure to address her as such," Etheldra said with a withering glare.

Bardoff, to his credit, didn't back down, so Etheldra merely turned and marched to the table.

"I know these things aren't popular," Bardoff said to Bev. "But there's *always* a reason for it. And if we had vendors out here who didn't have the right license, then—"

"You don't have to explain it to me," Bev said, holding up her hands. "I'm a neutral party."

He smiled, almost relieved, then took his plate to find a seat. Unfortunately, no one seemed to want him at their table, and Bev couldn't blame them. But she felt for Bardoff, so she beckoned him to follow her into the kitchen.

"You can sit here, if you like," Bev said. "I'm sure everyone's just hot under the collar because of all these rules. As soon as Warford completes his inspection of the town, things will settle."

"I'm sure the farmers will be fine, as will Sonny," Bardoff said. "It's not that much money to pay, you know. And it's only once a year. And—"

"I told you that you don't have to convince me of anything," Bev said with a knowing smile. "But it does sound like you need to convince yourself."

She left him there, returning to the front room, where the conversation had turned decidedly unfriendly toward the queen. At least three of the diners had had their vendor tables shut down, as they couldn't afford to pay the gold required to reopen. Those who could, or who'd already paid, said that the payment had completely cleared them out of whatever meager savings they'd had.

"Hope this town is in need of new tables," one of them said. "Otherwise, I'm in trouble."

Bev certainly felt for them and sent a few home with a couple extra slices of bread, just in case they couldn't come to dinner tomorrow. The dining room cleared out quickly, as no one was in a festive mood, and Bev set to cleaning up.

As she finished the first round of plates, the front door scraped open and Warford strolled in, once again surveying the room like he owned it. Bev had to muster every ounce of civility Wim McKee had taught her to keep her face neutral instead of launching into an angry tirade.

"Evening," Bev said. "There's a bit of food left, if you're hungry. But if you want to eat it hot, dinner's at six."

He crossed the room to inspect the remnants of

dinner. Bev half-expected him to ask if the butchers had their certifications and licenses, but he just fixed himself a plate and ate wordlessly. Bev couldn't help but notice he skipped the rosemary bread, and swallowed her annoyance.

"I'll be in the kitchen, if you need me," Bev said, instead of asking him what he had against rosemary.

She took her frustration out on the dishes, scrubbing them within an inch of their life and drying them furiously. She *really* shouldn't be so wrapped up in this contest. But she'd put in so much effort, time, experimentation. And to be thwarted by *one* judge who hated her signature herb… Well, that was just unfair.

There was a scratch and whine at the door, and Bev went to check on Biscuit. He was wagging his tail, though he didn't look too happy.

"What'd you find?" Bev asked.

He turned and walked out into the night. And Bev, of course, followed, stopping only to grab her trusty glowing stick.

Biscuit led her straight to Rustin's house. Bev had told Hendry she'd investigate in the morning, but if Biscuit had found something, that meant there was something magical afoot. Hendry had been right to be concerned.

The front door was unlocked—another concerning sign—and as Bev waved the glowing stick around, she found a house in complete disarray. A shelf of books was overturned, the kitchen table flipped over. A chair was broken, too. It looked like someone had been searching for something.

"Rustin, what in the world...?" Bev muttered. The sheriff was, well, to put it mildly, not the sharpest tool in the shed. He was affable, though, and never had a cross word to say about anyone. Hendry had kept him in his job because he did what she said and was enough of a deterrent to keep the peace in this already-peaceful town. What sort of nonsense had he gotten himself into?

And did it have anything to do with Andres's plan to get him fired?

Biscuit was in the kitchen, and when Bev joined him, she found a plank missing from his kitchen floor and a hole in the ground. Biscuit sniffed the hole and wagged his tail.

Something in Rustin's house had been magical.

"Well, that's certainly..." Bev cleared her throat. "I wonder what it could've been? And did Rustin take it, or did whoever took Rustin take whatever this was, too?"

Biscuit, of course, had no answer for her. But she did know someone who might.

~

It was late, but the light in the apartment above the butcher shop was still on. Bev rapped on the back door, hoping she wasn't interrupting, but this couldn't wait. She rapped again when she didn't get an answer then looked up when the window opened.

"Bev?" Vellora called, rubbing sleep from her eyes. "What in the world? It's so late."

"I need to speak with you," Bev said. "It's urgent."

"Me?" Ida poked her head out under Vellora's arm. "Is it about—"

"No. Erm." Goodness, Bev didn't know how to phrase this without raising Ida's suspicions. "I—"

"Say no more," Vellora said. "Give me a moment."

They disappeared from the window, which shut behind them, and Bev waited a few moments before Vellora came through the back door. She motioned for Bev to follow her, and led her far enough away from the butcher shop to escape prying ears.

"I'm sorry, but this couldn't wait," Bev said. "Rustin's gone missing."

Vellora opened and closed her mouth, seemingly perplexed. "He has? Why are you telling me?"

"I need to know if Andres is behind it before I go gallivanting about the town again," Bev said. "His house looks like it's been ransacked, and something magical was taken, if Biscuit's nose is to be believed. Hendry's beside herself with worry, which tells me something isn't quite right." Bev huffed when Vellora didn't respond right away.

"Andres said that he cursed people and framed Bernard just to get Rustin fired. Or the sheriff's position to be vacant. Either way—"

"I don't have any information about that," Vellora said. "But...to be fair, I don't have any information *period*. My job is pretty simple."

"Yes, keep your head down."

She cracked a half-smile. "And watch you. Make sure you don't go spilling any beans."

Bev glared at her. "A fine job."

"An important one," Vellora said. "And one I'm glad to take, because I know you, Bev. And I know you're not going to do anything to jeopardize our mission."

Bev sniffed. "Well, I'm letting *you* know that my next stop is to tell Karolina that Rustin's gone missing. So, if you'd like to get a message to Andres, you might tell him that."

"Do you have to tell her?" Vellora asked. "He's been moping about town for weeks now. Maybe he just decided to leave."

Bev shook her head. "That's not what it looks like." She clicked her tongue. "Why was it so important for the sheriff position to be vacant?"

"I don't know, and I mean that," Vellora said. "Andres is very stingy with his plans, and people only know what they need to do their jobs. Especially now, with Her Majesty riding into town any day now. If any of us gets caught, or questioned, or given a truth potion, then we only know our part."

Bev begrudgingly supposed that made sense. "Is he around? Andres?"

"I haven't seen him since that night," Vellora said. "But I've got a way I can get a message to him about Rustin."

Bev released a slow breath. "Do you think he's planning to do something to the queen? Take advantage of her being out here at the Harvest Festival? I hope he's not bringing his war to Pigsend. The town won't survive."

Vellora was quiet a long time. "I don't *think* so. In the first place, the queen would have *more* protection around her here, being so far away from Queen's Capital. Especially with all the rumors flying around about Andres. If he's going to do something like that, he'd make sure he'd be successful—no mistakes."

Bev exhaled, the tight knot in her stomach that had been in her stomach for weeks relaxing. "Thank goodness. I'm trying to win the breadmaking contest this year."

Vellora let out a belly laugh, and it loosened the rest of the tension in Bev's stomach. "I think you're safe, at least from him. But I'm hearing all manner of complaining from Ida tonight. What is that judge doing, shutting down the farmers' market?"

"He says he's within his purview," Bev said.

"Never thought I'd miss Petula Banks, but at least she had some sense of gray areas. Warford is all black and white and no exceptions."

"Now you understand why we're doing what we're doing," Vellora said gently. "Imagine Warford finding out about Ida's strength. Do you think he'd look the other way? Or do you think he'd see she had a small amount of magic and throw her in jail?" She gestured to the dark. "She gave Bernard no quarter."

"Because Andres set him up," Bev reminded her. "I've half a mind to march down to Lower Pigsend and tell him what really happened."

Vellora smiled at her, and there was a little pity in it. "I know you can't see the forest for the trees, but one day, this will all make perfect sense. For now..." She shook her head. "For now, do what you must about Rustin. But I have a feeling Karolina won't care about him one bit."

Chapter Six

"Why should I care what happens to that no-good cod's head?"

The next morning, after seeing off her guests for the day, Bev sought out Karolina in the town square and informed her about Rustin. Bev shouldn't have been surprised, especially after Vellora's warning the night before, but the severity of Karolina's words still took her aback.

"He's a citizen in this town," Bev said, after a moment. "Sheriff or not, he's still a member of the community. And it looks like he's been kidnapped."

"Or, he's a depressed slob who left town," Karolina said. "Listen, I don't have time for your nonsense today, innkeeper. When the new Pigsend

Sheriff arrives, I'm sure they'll be eager to look into it."

"New sheriff?" Bev blinked. "When should we expect them?"

"Probably next spring," she said, walking away.

Bev stayed where she was, watching Karolina march off, barking orders at this vendor and that. As had been the case during dinner the night before, no one looked happy, and the number of vendors operating was *much* smaller than it had been the day before. Thankfully, those who'd come to town for the festival itself seemed oblivious to the tension and politics plaguing the vendors and contestants. They, at least, were enjoying themselves, and Bev hoped they had enough coin in their pocket to change the fortunes of the downtrodden vendors.

Since Karolina was a dead end, Bev headed for the town hall to find Hendry. The jam-making contest was in progress, with Warford once again interrogating every single entrant, though today he was joined by another man who was cut from the same cloth. Bev had to assume that was the second judge he'd sent for and remembered a little moodily that she'd have to shuffle her guests around to make room for him. Ira had said he'd be fine doubling up on a room, but she'd still have to find a spot to put him.

But those problems were for when she returned to the inn. Now, she scanned the town hall for

Mayor Hendry. Her office was empty, but Bev finally spotted her sitting in a far-off corner, watching the proceedings with a thin-lipped grimace. No one was anywhere near her, so Bev walked over to sit beside her.

"How's it going in here?" Bev asked, nodding to the contest.

"The same as everywhere else," Hendry said evenly.

"That bad, huh?" Bev muttered, glancing at the roof. "Is that the new judge?"

She nodded. "Fitzwilliam Bombadom."

"That's a name," Bev said. "Tell me he's got a nickname."

"Not that I'm aware of," Hendry said. "But I haven't been able to speak with him at length. He arrived just in time to judge the jam."

Bev nodded and gazed at the front of the room. Warford had moved on to the next entrant, picking up the jar of jam and visually inspecting it before asking them questions. Bev only caught the gist of it but had to assume he was asking about the source of the fruit, sugar, and jars themselves.

"Was there something you needed?" Hendry asked.

"I told Karolina about Rustin going missing."

"I'm guessing she was uninterested," Hendry said without prompting.

Bev turned to her. "How did you know?"

"Because she was the first person I spoke to about it," Hendry said with a knowing smile. "I *am* trying to keep things off your plate, Bev. But when she voiced her opinion on the matter, I decided to ask you to look into it. Or rather, your *dog*." She swallowed, some of her facade cracking. "Have you found anything?"

"Biscuit led me to his house," Bev said. "Did you notice that gaping hole in the kitchen floor?"

"No." Hendry turned to her. "What are you talking about?"

Bev told her what she'd found, and how Biscuit had been very interested in the dirt under the house. Hendry slowly shook her head. "There wasn't anything of the sort when I was there. The only things I saw were the overturned bookshelf and furniture." She tapped her finger on her chin. "Maybe someone wanted to get Rustin out of the house so they could retrieve something they weren't supposed to have."

"What's Rustin's story?" Bev asked. "I mean, before I came to town."

"He grew up in Pigsend," she said. "He's five years younger than me, so I never really interacted much with him outside of the schoolhouse. After he was done with that, he left to join Her Majesty's forces. Was gone a few years, through the war, too, but when it was over, he came back to Pigsend, and I appointed him sheriff."

"Why?"

"Well, in the first place, he was the only candidate. During the war, *everyone* who served either the queen or king was sent to the front lines. There wasn't a sheriff to be seen in these parts for almost five years. So when Rustin walked through my front door with his credentials, asking for a job, I gave him the position."

"I didn't realize he was in the war, too," Bev said.

"Well..." Hendry cleared her throat. "Lots of people who did lots of things in the war didn't exactly see the front lines. Rustin certainly didn't have any stories about it, nor did he show any signs of the sorts of trauma you see from those who actively participated."

Bev supposed that made sense. "Did he say anything strange recently? Mention anyone was after him, or anything about his past?"

"No," she said with a sigh. "And to be honest, with the way he's been carrying on, if I hadn't seen the state of his house, I'd say he'd just left town. But he was a neat fellow, and his house was always immaculate. Not to mention all his clothes were still in his dresser. Food was still in his pantry, too. And now, with this mysterious hole in his kitchen, too, I can't imagine he left willingly."

Bev rubbed her chin. "Maybe it really was wrong place, wrong time. Do you remember who lived in his house before he did? They might've been the ones to bury whatever Biscuit scented."

"Goodness, who lived there...?" Hendry thought for a moment then shook her head. "I can't remember. Max would know. He keeps all those records." She sighed, nodding to the front of the room, where Warford was arguing with Mandy Nowak about the source of her berries. "Either way, I've got my hands full keeping the townsfolk from rioting. If we can get through this festival without someone throwing a right hook at that judge, I'll eat my hat."

"Our Harvest Festival judges seem to want to stick their fingers into everything," Bev said. "Yesterday, he told me *Sonny* didn't have the right registration to run his mill."

"I've taken care of that," Hendry said. "Sonny's licenses and fees have been paid for."

Bev stared at her. "Really? Why would you—"

"We can't not have a miller, Bev," Hendry said. "Etheldra would skin me alive if I stood in the way of your breadmaking."

That was true. "What about the farmers' market? Can you get that back on?" Bev said.

Hendry's nostrils flared. "That, unfortunately, I can't do anything about. The only saving grace is that we're at the end of the season, and the farmers were going to pack it in soon enough anyway. Hopefully, by next year, everyone will have their paperwork in order, and there won't be a problem."

"I just can't imagine a reason the queen insists everyone be so…*official*," Bev said. "And to pay so much money. She certainly can't care that much about the type of wheat a miller processes or the source of a Harvest Festival jam."

Hendry shifted uncomfortably. "Who knows what goes on in the mind of a queen? I certainly do things as mayor that make people scratch their heads. But there's always…" She pursed her lips as Mandy's raised voice echoed in the space. "…always a reason."

"Five years I've been second place. Now I'm not even allowed to compete! This festival is a sham!" Mandy cried to Ida. "Who does this guy think he is?"

"Her Majesty's official representative," Warford said, his chin lifting in the air. "And if you continue to cause a commotion, I'll have no choice but to find Ms. Hunter and have her speak with you."

The unsaid threat hung in the air, and Mandy's face paled. Finally, Ida's gentle tugging on her arm caught her attention, and with tears in her eyes, she allowed herself to be led away from the others.

Hendry sighed as she rose. "I should probably walk with her a spell. Let me know what you hear from Max, Bev. I'd like my sheriff back, even if he isn't exactly employed by me anymore."

Bev lingered in the town hall to watch the conclusion of the judging, but no one else seemed to cross Mr. Warford the way Mandy had. At the end of the contest, he'd disqualified three people for trivial reasons then selected five to continue to the final judging in a few days. Ida returned midway through the judging, and Bev pulled her aside to ask what had happened to Mandy.

"Oh, who knows?" Ida said, rubbing her forehead. "It's been like this with every single contest so far. I've tried to give fair warning to everyone, but even when I think everything's exactly correct, Warford comes up with something else to ding them on. We can't win, you know?" She also looked on the verge of tears. "And I've spent the last two days trying to assuage all the vendors who've been told to go on their way. Many of them want compensation for their time, and I've had to tell them I don't have the budget to give them all what they're asking for. It's been an absolute nightmare."

Bev could only imagine. "Did you hear about Rustin?"

"Oh, goodness, what's he done now?" Ida said, her entire body slumping.

"He's… You know what? Don't worry about it," Bev said. "It's nothing. Sorry I mentioned it."

"I've got to get up to David Frank's house," Ida said, glancing at the large clock on the wall. "Just to triple check the livestock pens are *regulation sized.*"

She paused. "Are you sure there's nothing I need to know about Rustin?"

Bev shook her head. "Nope. Go on. I've got things covered here."

There wasn't any relief on Ida's face, only the tension that seemed everywhere Bev looked. The day was wearing on, and Bev had to pop across the square to talk with Max before heading back to the inn. She left the quiet town hall, weaving through the bustling crowd, and opened the heavy door to the town library. There, she found Max Sterling scribbling in a book. He looked up when she walked in, his smile tinged with the same tension Bev saw almost everywhere else.

"Bev! To what do I owe the pleasure?"

"I wanted to ask about a town record," Bev said. "Who lived in Sheriff Rustin's house before he did?"

"Why?" Max frowned. "Has something happened?"

She told him, in brief, about Rustin's disappearance, and the strange hole in the ground, leaving out the part about Biscuit finding magical residue. Max favored the kingside in the war, as evidenced by his shelf full of illegal magical books in his office, but she couldn't be too careful.

"Goodness. Poor fellow. He took his sacking pretty hard," Max said. "Though I can't say he was doing a wonderful job here as sheriff, he's always been kind. But perhaps if he'd done his job with

Bernard, we might not have gotten cursed, you know?"

Bev nodded. Max was one of the curse victims, and Bev hated that she couldn't tell him exactly what had happened to him or why. "In any case, I'm hoping if I find out who lived in his house before him, it might help me figure out what happened to him."

"You don't happen to remember what year he moved back to town, do you?" Max asked.

"Hendry said it was six years ago," Bev said. "Same year I arrived."

Max nodded and disappeared into the stacks. Bev kept a wary eye on him, as the last time she'd asked him for something, he'd ended up cursed. But today, he brought her a heavy book that was covered in dust and hoisted it onto the counter with a loud *thump*.

"Let's see what we have." He flipped through the pages quickly, until about midway through the book, then he smiled and turned it around. "Here's every Pigsend resident and where they live."

Bev scanned the list, looking for the intersection where Rustin lived. Of course, things in Pigsend weren't all that organized, so some of the descriptions were of the house instead of the cross streets, but Bev scanned it several times only to come up empty.

"It's not here," Bev said. "Maybe he didn't move

into his house until later?"

They tried the next year, and to Bev's surprise, found Rustin's house listed under his own name. When she compared the two residency lists, she confirmed Rustin's house did not exist when he arrived but it did exist after.

"Suppose that makes sense," Max said. "There were a few plots here and there that hadn't been built on yet. Maybe Earl built his house for him. You could ask him or Jane about it."

"I might do that," Bev said, though she didn't really see the need. If Rustin's house had been built on the plot, then whatever the people who took him were looking for might've been buried there years before, and Rustin could've been the unfortunate soul living on top of it. "Thank you, Max. Appreciate your insight, as always."

"You be careful out there, Bev. I'm hearing lots of complaints about the queen's people being more ornery than usual," he said, his face turning gray. "They're running about town, asking all the business owners if they have licenses to operate. If they don't, they're making them pay their weight in gold to stay open."

"So I've heard," Bev said. "But it's just the Harvest Festival, isn't it?"

He shook his head. "I heard that Mr. Warford over at Wilda Murtagh's shop the other day. Apparently even *candlemakers* need licenses, per the queen. Can you believe such a silly thing?"

Bev could. "Well, I've got some gold saved up if they come asking for my license. But I daresay I've never heard a word about it, so they can't blame me for not having one."

"I don't think anyone in town's heard a word about it," he said. "And between you, me, and the books, I think they're just making things up to collect gold."

"Surely, Her Majesty will put a stop to it when she arrives," Bev said.

"Hmph." He adjusted his tunic. "Maybe I should be out of town when she comes calling to the library."

Bev nodded to the open door to his office. "You may want to—erm—hide some of those books you've got in there."

"Already ahead of you," he said. "I've got them stashed safely away in my apartment upstairs."

Bev didn't think that was a good idea. "I could take them for you, if you like. I know a safer place." It came with a six-foot moleman, but Max didn't need to know that. "If they're the sort of books that could incriminate you—"

He waved her off. "There are still laws in this country. They can't just inspect my home without cause, you know. And what cause would they have to arrest a simple librarian and town archivist?"

Chapter Seven

Bev could think of many reasons, but Max couldn't be convinced to part with his contraband. And it would be a struggle for Bev to find a time when she could lug the books to Merv's house without being seen. As it was, she'd avoided visiting just to keep Karolina from asking questions—not that the soldier had been paying her much attention.

Still, she had something of an answer from Max. Rustin's house was constructed for the sheriff, which meant either the sheriff himself had buried whatever magical object he'd had under his floorboard *or* someone else had, thinking the vacant lot would remain that way forever. Either way, it didn't bring her any closer to an answer.

She walked out of the library back into the busy square, but didn't make it far before she saw a familiar face. Vicky Hamblin, Allen's ex-fiancée, stood next to one of the jewelry vendor slots, talking animatedly with her former boss, seamstress Apolinary McGraw. Vicky looked absolutely radiant and brightened even more when she spotted Bev approaching.

"Bev! Goodness, it's so wonderful to see you!" Vicky bounded over and enveloped Bev in a tight hug. "You look incredible. The whole town looks incredible. I've missed Pigsend so much."

"How's life in Sheepsburg?" Bev asked.

"Oh, it's absolutely wonderful," Vicky said. "I was overjoyed when the boys came, too. They've got a nice little apartment together near the university. I was just telling Apolinary that I've almost got my seamstress shop set up. I've been mending clothes out of my own apartment, just trying to get a name for myself before I go into business officially."

"That's wonderful, but…do you need a shop?" Bev didn't know how to phrase it. "Didn't your inheritance…?"

On her wedding-day-that-wasn't, Vicky and her brother Grant had been informed of a sizable amount of money waiting in an account for them, but only if Vicky married before her twenty-first birthday. The younger of her two aunts, Lucy, had been keeping the account secret from her, and had gone so far as to curse Vicky's wedding to ensure it didn't happen, so that the money would go to Lucy. When Vicky and Allen had ultimately decided they weren't ready for marriage yet anyway, Vicky's other aunt Marion had promised to work to lift the stipulation.

"Yes, the inheritance is still there," Vicky said. "But if there's one thing I learned, it's never to take *anything* for granted. This money may not last forever, and I'd certainly be up Pigsend Creek if I ran out one day. Best to keep my seamstress skills, and also build myself a business."

"Allen mentioned you were attending university," Bev said.

"Oh, I am," she said with a bright smile. "Taking lots of courses on running a business. Just applying them a little faster."

"You're planning to stay in Sheepsburg, then?" Bev said, thinking of Allen. He'd intimated they'd been writing to one another, and he seemed hopeful they might rekindle their relationship one day.

"As of right now, yes," she said with a shrug. "But one never knows what the future will hold. For now, the boys and I are happy building our lives there. But Pigsend will always be home. They're just as happy as I am to be back in town."

Bev smiled. "Are Grant and PJ here, too?"

"Oh, yes! They came home with me," Vicky

said, nodding emphatically. "The timing of the festival coincided with a planned break in our studies, so it all worked out. I know Pip and Holly were eager to see PJ again."

Bev nodded, though PJ's parents were probably less eager with Karolina Hunter in town—not to mention Her Majesty's imminent arrival. Though the festival had entered its second day, and there hadn't been any signs of the queen yet. Bev had to assume she was just planning on being fashionably late.

"How are they enjoying school?" Bev asked.

"PJ's taken to it like a duck to water," Vicky said. "Grant…well, he has to maintain a certain grade level in order to continue *attending* school. And *his* inheritance is predicated on his completion of his studies, so…"

"Was that in your inheritance, too?" Bev said. "I thought you had to get married?"

"Oh, that whole stipulation's been removed, thankfully," Vicky said, waving her hand. "But I enforced my own with Grant, with help from my *dear* Aunt Marion. She's been such an invaluable resource as we settle in to Sheepsburg."

Bev bit her tongue. *Dear* hadn't been the adjective Vicky had used last spring. "What does she think of your seamstress shop idea?"

"She's happy to see my business sense," Vicky said, though the tightness around her mouth told

Bev Marion perhaps thought mending clothes wasn't the best job for a woman of Vicky's wealth. "But going back to Grant, as I'm the eldest, I'm in control of the accounts right now. So it's my say. Marion, of course, was absolutely on board with the decision to tie Grant's inheritance to his studies. She said she's seen so many people squander their money away and end up without any way to support themselves. Though, *ahem*, I think she'd rather I go into a different industry, I told her mending and making clothes is what I know, and I'm confident I can make my way with it."

"I'm so happy to hear things are going well," Bev said with a smile. "I've got to head back to the inn to get going on dinner. If you catch up with the boys, tell them to pop by the inn. I'd love to see them and hear about their studies. I know Bardoff would be eager as well."

Heartened by her impromptu visit with Vicky, Bev arrived back at the inn and remembered she needed to swap around some of her guests' rooms. She peered into her book, running her finger along the list of names. Ira, of course, had volunteered to move, but perhaps Mandisa Munson would be fine sharing with Ms. Hann. Mandisa had been one of the few jam-makers who'd made it to the next round of the contest, and she and Ms. Hann had gotten along the night before at dinner. The other guests were all couples, so they wouldn't be able to add a third. Bev checked her laundry stores to make sure she had fresh sheets to add to whichever room would be prepared for Mr. Bombadom, before returning downstairs just as the front door opened.

Bev smiled, readying herself to direct whomever had come by to wherever they were looking to go, but instead let out a yelp of happiness when PJ Norris walked through the door. He, too, brightened when he saw Bev, and hurried to meet her in the middle of the room.

"Oh, Bev, it's so good to see you!" he said, squeezing her tightly.

"And you!" She stepped back to look at him. "Goodness, have you grown? It's only been a few months since you left."

"Maybe. Vicky's had to let out some of my pants lately." He grinned. "You look shorter, too."

"Come, come. I've got to get dinner going, but I want to catch up."

PJ followed her into the kitchen, where he helped her peel potatoes. He told her all about Sheepsburg and the university there. He described the courses he loved, skimmed over those he didn't, and spoke about the mischief he and Grant were getting into.

"Valta was certainly morose about you two leaving her behind," Bev said. "At least when I spoke to her a few weeks ago."

"We lobbied as hard as we could, but her parents wouldn't hear of it," PJ said with a shake of his head.

"And how's…" Bev's gaze dropped to PJ's chest, where presumably an amulet was hanging. "Any news on that front?"

"I got a letter from the grannies," PJ said with a smile. "Haven't a clue how they knew I was in Sheepsburg, or that I was going to university, but they wrote to tell me to study hard and learn a lot. There wasn't a return address on the letter, so I'm not sure where they were. Suppose it's for the best that they keep a low profile."

Bev nodded. The trio of old ladies were also dragon shifters and had been in Pigsend to find PJ before he turned into a full-fledged dragon. "Speaking of, I know your parents told you—"

"About all the soldiers in town?" He nodded. "Mom wasn't happy to see me, but I told her I wasn't going to do anything to draw attention to myself. There are so many people around, you know? But Grant's not willing to stay very long. He's staying with his father's cousin Dane Sterling. That's a far walk out of town, and he never got along with his father's side. I don't think he'd be sad to head back to Sheepsburg early."

"I'm glad you stopped by, in any case," Bev said. "And I'm even more glad to hear things are going well in Sheepsburg. It's been quiet around here—"

"Not per my father's letters," PJ said with a knowing look. "Something about blackmail letters and curses?"

"Well, fair point," Bev said. "And now that you mention it, Sheriff Rustin's gone missing."

"Really? Do you need my help looking into anything?" PJ asked.

"I'm somewhat at a dead end," Bev said. "I had Biscuit sniff around town looking for him, but all he did was take me to Rustin's house, where I found the hole in the floor. Rustin was the only one who lived in that house, so either someone buried something in that plot before the house was built, or..."

"I doubt Rustin had anything worth digging up," PJ said. "Unless maybe it was a sack of gold."

Bev stopped, turning to look at him. "You know, I hadn't considered that."

"Maybe he'd buried his savings under his kitchen, forgot where it was, then destroyed his house looking for it," PJ said.

"Yes, except... Hendry said all his clothes were still in his house," Bev said. "And there was food in the pantry. So if his goal was to leave then wouldn't he have taken all his things with him?"

"I don't know. If I wanted a new life, I might leave most of my stuff behind, too." He shrugged. "Not as if we brought much to Sheepsburg, either. Makes things easier that way."

"I suppose." Bev had certainly shown up in town without anything but the shirt on her back, but that had been a special situation.

PJ stayed until almost five, peeling and chopping and helping Bev get things ready for dinner. But he had to leave, as his mother demanded him home before the festival activities concluded. Bev gave him another hug, and told him to write to her, and he promised he would.

At six, Bev brought out dinner to a crowd that was once again half the usual size. Though everyone looked to be in a marginally better mood, that was quickly squashed by the appearance of Warford and Bombadom.

"Good evening, Ms. Bev," Warford said. "As I instructed earlier, Mr. Bombadom is in need of his own lodgings."

"Yes, erm, I haven't had a chance to discuss it with the others, yet," Bev said, looking around the room for Ira, Mandisa, or Gena. "If you'll give me a moment—"

"I was under the assumption that this was the sort of inn Her Majesty could rely on to accommodate her representatives," Bombadom said, his voice low and without any ounce of friendliness.

"It is," Bev began slowly. "I just need a moment to confirm with—"

"Then I expect to be given a room key." He extended his hand. "Without any more of this back and forth."

The hum of conversation went quiet. Bev forced a smile onto her face. "I understand that you're in need of a room. Unfortunately, I had both judges sharing a space. I'm, of course, happy to accommodate your request. But before I do, I must confirm with the guests currently occupying the room that they're willing to move. Because while you and Mr. Warford are valued members of Her Majesty's service, no guest at the Weary Dragon is more important than anyone else."

Bombadom bristled, but before he could argue, the front door opened, and Ira, Mandisa, and Gena walked in together.

"Now, see?" Bev said, gesturing to them. "Let me confer with these three. I'm sure we can come up with a reasonable solution."

Bev felt every single eye in the room on her as she approached Ira, Gena, and Mandisa. The discussion was quick, with Mandisa almost predicting what Bev was going to ask and agreeing to move her things into Gena's room. The transfer was smooth, and Bev changed the sheets as fast as she could. When she returned to the front room, it had completely cleared of diners. Even Etheldra had left, perhaps not wanting to get on the judges' bad side before the initial pie-making contest in the morning.

"Thank you for your patience," Bev said,

handing over Mandisa's key. "It is appreciated."

Neither one said a word, and Bombadom picked up his suitcase and marched upstairs. Bev jumped when the doors slammed, but was grateful, at least, that it wasn't a bigger fiasco. She'd dealt with all manner of guests at the Weary Dragon over the years, but there was something about Warford's threats to call in Karolina and Bombadom's tone that made Bev uneasy. Any other soldier might have some room for gray, but Karolina held a grudge.

Bev let all that worry go as she gathered dishes and brought them back into the kitchen for washing. Biscuit settled in next to the hearth, and soon, she lost herself to the rhythmic movements of dunking plates into sudsy water and rinsing them.

She was nearly finished with the entire effort when Biscuit lifted his head, nose twitching. Not a moment later, there was a soft knock on the back door. Bev frowned at her laelaps then walked to the door, wiping her wet hands on her apron.

Grant, Vicky's brother, stood on the other side, wringing his hands. "Hey, Bev. Sorry to bother you so late."

"No, no, come in," Bev said, reading the concern on his face. "Are you all right? Has something happened to PJ?"

"Nah, he's fine," Grant said, shifting from one foot to another. "It's actually just…" He licked his lips. "I'm staying with my old man's cousin, Dane

Sterling."

Bev nodded. "PJ told me."

"This morning, he told me he was going out to the festival, to make myself at home, whatever." He rubbed the back of his head. "And he said he'd be back this evening. But I got back to his house, and waited, and, erm…well, he hasn't come back yet." Grant met Bev's gaze. "PJ told me Rustin went missing. Maybe whoever took Rustin took Dane too?"

"I don't think…" Bev began slowly. Then she thought better of it. "How about this: go on back to Dane's house for the night. If he doesn't come back, I'll head over and check things out with you in the morning. Maybe he's still looking at the vendor market. Or maybe he…" Bev was about to suggest maybe he'd had too much to drink, but the only place to get a drink was the Weary Dragon, and she hadn't seen him tonight. "In any case, let's not worry ourselves too much until there's something to worry about."

Chapter Eight

A whole year of investigating these curiosities had made Bev paranoid, she decided as she rose the next morning and did her chores. People came and went during the Harvest Festival. It wasn't uncommon for people to stay out too late, grab a spot under a tree somewhere, and get home in the morning. But, like Hendry, Grant never showed concern for anyone except himself. For him to come to Bev meant he really felt something was wrong.

So once she finished her morning chores, and saw off her guests (unsurprisingly, Warford and Bombadom weren't interested in a morning muffin *or* conversation), Bev and Biscuit headed south to Dane Sterling's house. She held out hope that the trip would be pointless, that she'd knock on the door and Dane would answer, but it was Grant's worried face that met her on the front steps.

"Still not back," he said. "You didn't see him around town, did you?"

"Can't say I did," Bev said.

"It's not like him. He doesn't drink or do anything like this," Grant continued. "I mean, we weren't close, but that's because Vic and I tried to live here for a bit. He was too wooden for us. Get up at the crack of dawn. Tend to the fields. No lunch until all the chores are done. Just real strict, you know?"

Bev, who lived that life as the proprietor of the Weary Dragon, could see how someone like Grant could chafe under that rule, so she just nodded.

"So for him to be gone like this... It's just not normal," Grant continued, gesturing to the house. "What d'ya think happened with Rustin? PJ didn't say."

"Because I don't know," Bev said, looking around the house. Unlike Rustin's, which looked like there'd been a struggle, Dane's house was neat and tidy. Nothing was out of place. There was even a basket of food on the table. "He didn't leave a note or anything?"

"Not that I found," Grant said before frowning. "What's your dog doing?"

Biscuit had found a door off the kitchen and

was scratching at it.

"I'm not sure," Bev said. "Maybe he scented something." The door was unlocked, and when she opened it, there were stairs up to what appeared to be an attic. "What's up there?"

"No clue," Grant said. "Vic and I shared a room down here. Dane's bedroom is down here, too. Didn't know there was an upstairs."

Biscuit was already halfway up the stairs, his tail upright. They led to an attic that was sparsely filled with dusty crates. Biscuit marched forward purposefully until he disappeared behind a pair of stacked crates. Bev and Grant followed and found a closed trunk.

"What d'ya reckon is in here?" Grant asked.

"I don't know, but..." Bev eyed the trunk. It had less dust on it than everything else in the attic, and when she inspected it closer, she spotted fingerprints. "I think it's been opened recently."

She found the clasp unlocked and carefully lifted the top. Inside were tattered tunics in red and black, a blanket, and not much else. Even when Bev and Grant emptied the contents completely, there was nothing left.

"What do you think he's so interested in?" Grant asked. Biscuit was still sniffing the case, his paws perched on the edge. "Maybe there was some old bacon in here or something."

"Maybe so," Bev said. "Or there was something

magical here."

"Magical?" Grant looked at Biscuit. "Can he smell that?"

"He's not a dog," Bev said. Grant kept PJ's secret, so she could trust him with Biscuit's. "He's a laelaps. It's kind of a magical sniffer."

"Oh, well, that explains why he likes PJ so much," Grant said. "He doesn't transform into anything, does he?"

"Not to my knowledge," Bev said. "As much as I hate to admit it, it seems there's a pattern here. Someone goes missing, and something appears to be taken from their house." She pawed at the fabrics again, willing them to reveal their secrets. "And you're sure Dane wouldn't have just left? He's not out working in the fields, or…?"

"No, I'm sure of it," Grant said. "What reason would he have to leave? Especially with me here."

Bev chewed her lip. Two people now missing, two people without anything to connect them. Which was exactly how it had seemed with the cursing just a month before. The goal then had been random attacks. Was Andres using the same strategy now? And to what end?

"Stay close to the house, in case he comes back," Bev said. "I'm going to go ask some questions and see what I can find."

"Bev…" Grant sighed. "I don't like being involved in one of these. I mean, being on the other side of it. I liked it when PJ was crashing houses and breathing smoke, but I don't like having to worry about Dane."

Bev chuckled. "I know what you mean."

~

Bev's first stop was across the street from the inn, as she hoped Vellora had an answer from Andres about Rustin's disappearance. She didn't know how quickly messages came and went, but she had to assume quickly. Still, her face fell when she walked through the front door and was once again face-to-face with Hans.

"Hey, Bev!" he said, entirely too happily for Bev's liking. "Are you here to pick up your meat for dinner?"

"Where's Vellora?" Bev asked, looking around.

"She's out doing meat deliveries," he said. "But I've got your order all ready. It's chicken tonight, if that's all right—"

"Did Andres do something with Dane Sterling?" Bev demanded.

Hans frowned, looking honestly concerned. "What's wrong with Dane?"

Bev remembered almost too late that Hans and Freddie were Dane's neighbors, along with Trent Scrawl. "Grant's staying with him and said Dane never came home last night. Wasn't home this morning, either."

"That's not like him," Hans said with a shake of

his head.

"Did Andres do something with him?" Bev repeated.

"I don't know... I mean, I don't *think* so. He's a farmer, isn't he? He's not been in any of our conversations with Andres. I don't really know his politics, either. I think his cousin—Grant and Vicky's father—went to fight for the kingside, but other than that..."

"Is this some kind of plot to get someone fired again?" Bev asked. "Because Sheriff Rustin is *also* missing."

"That's...well, I doubt we had anything to do with that," Hans said with a laugh. "He's not employed by the queen anymore, so we don't have any quarrel with him."

"Do you know why Andres wanted him fired?"

"I don't," Hans said. "But I don't think it was about Rustin. He just wanted the sheriff position vacant. Now it is."

"Karolina Hunter is the de facto sheriff. Is this his ploy to get her gone, too? Disappear people in town instead of cursing them to sleep?"

Hans swallowed, his cheeks turning pink. "The townsfolk were *fine*, Bev."

"They weren't, but that's neither here nor there," Bev said impatiently. "If he's trying to get her fired, there are better ways to do it than kidnapping people."

"I don't think that's his end goal," Hans said, after a moment's thought. "When we spoke about it, he was under the assumption that Karolina was just a short-term solution. That she was going to move on after the Harvest Festival, and the position would once again be vacant." He swallowed. "He didn't *say* this, but my assumption is he's going to slide in someone allied to us."

"How's he going to do that?" Bev asked.

"Pigsend is pretty far removed from everything. Pretty easy to intercept a letter, forge a new one. He's done it before," Hans said. "He always has a plan, you know?"

"I know, which is why I'm here asking about Rustin and Dane," Bev said. "If not to get Karolina fired, then why is he kidnapping people?"

"Now, I don't know that it's him," Hans said. "It could be totally unrelated. I mean, Dane and Rustin don't exactly run in the same circles. Dane could've just decided to go for a holiday—"

"Grant says Dane didn't give him any indication that he was leaving town. Said he was going to the Harvest Festival to check things out then never came home."

"That's a pickle, then," Hans said, shaking his head. Then, as if the whole ordeal were as banal as a rainstorm, he brightened and headed toward the back. "Let me get your meat order so you can get going on dinner. It always smells so good when I'm walking home, I'm tempted to stop in. But Fred likes me home to eat. It's about the only time we get to spend together at the moment."

"And what's your husband doing?" Bev asked, suspicious.

"It's harvest time," Hans called. "He's finishing up in the fields and getting them ready for winter."

Bev tried to look neutral. "Surprised he let you off for the week to help Vellora."

"Oh, I'm usually in the way," Hans said as he walked out of the back room with three prepared chickens. "He does the farming, and I sell our wares in Middleburg. And, of course, to Sonny."

Bev clicked her tongue. "You heard what happened to him, right?"

Hans nodded. "The queen's people are about as ruthless in Middleburg when it comes to wheat. I mean, Hendry was able to negotiate so we could sell thrice what we were selling, but we have to have these licenses and whatnot. It's all just a gold grab from the queen." He sighed. "That's why Fred wanted to run for mayor. Try to alleviate some of the pressure on the farmers."

"Well, I hate to inform you, but Her Majesty's pressure is expanding," Bev said. "I wouldn't be surprised if Warford came barging in here, asking for the Witzels' license to sell meat."

"Or the inn," Hans said. "I'm sure she has some specific criteria for how an inn should be run, too."

Bev exhaled. She didn't even want to think about it. "I suppose I'd better be getting these in the oven."

"I'll get that message to Andres," Hans said. "I mean, after all you've been through, we owe you that much. If we're involved, I'll let you know."

Unsatisfied, but without any other avenues to press with Hans, Bev took her meat across the street and started preparations to get it in the oven. As she'd learned during the cursing episode, just because one of Andres's people didn't know about his plans didn't mean they weren't happening behind the scenes. She once again took her frustrations out on dinner, getting the chickens in the oven and peeling the potatoes with more force than was necessary. As she was tipping the last of the spuds into the pan, she remembered that, for once, the town actually had someone *else* who could handle these things. Karolina hadn't been interested in Rustin's disappearance, but she might be keener to investigate now that a second person had gone missing.

With dinner set, Bev headed back to the festival to search for her. She checked the square, the town hall, and even the tea shop and schoolhouse, but didn't find her. Finally, one of the vendors had something to report.

"She's up north, checking out the livestock

pen."

Bev frowned. Why would Karolina want to investigate the livestock pen?

Without any other ideas, she headed north. There was a crowd up here, too, though the livestock judging wouldn't occur until tomorrow. Some of the folks had already put their cows and pigs into the holding area, and those gathered were comparing who might have a chance at winning tomorrow.

Bev scanned the area, looking at every face until she finally saw Karolina. The soldier was walking *into* town, as if she'd just been…

…at the dark forest, north of town.

Bev clicked her tongue. What could Karolina be hiding now?

"Ms. Hunter, excuse me!" Bev called, catching her as she walked by. "Hello, I need to speak with you."

"I'm busy."

"Yes, but I think you'll want to hear this," Bev said, jogging up to walk beside her. "We've had another citizen go missing."

"Riveting."

Bev frowned. "Aren't you the sheriff? This is clearly a pattern. You've got to investigate it."

"I don't have to *do* anything, especially not on your orders," she snapped. "I think you forget your place, innkeeper."

Bev pursed her lips. "What's in the dark forest,

then?"

"Nothing, if I have my way," Karolina said. "What? You think I'd leave such a hotbed of magical activity alone with Her Majesty's arrival?"

"So her arrival is imminent?" Bev asked. "When? Today? Tomorrow? The festival's already halfway over—"

"You'll know when you see her," Karolina said.

"Fine, then what are you going to do about the missing people? I'm sure Her Majesty would be concerned to know people are missing."

"I told you. It's not my problem."

Bev stopped, letting Karolina disappear into the crowd of people. She put her hands on her hips, pursing her lips and letting an angry breath out. She'd always been flustered that Rustin wasn't a better sheriff, but at least he *tried*. Tried and failed, usually, but he would've at least stopped to listen to Bev's concerns.

Still, there was one government official who might listen, and Bev found her working away in her office. "Yes, Bev, what can I do for you?" Hendry said, without looking up.

"Dane Sterling's missing now," Bev said.

Hendry lifted her gaze. "Goodness. Well, inform our sheriff. I'm sure she'll be happy to look into it."

"She didn't care," Bev said, sinking into the chair across from Hendry. "Said she was too busy preparing for the queen." She gestured to the air.

"When is that woman going to show up, anyway?"

"Only she knows," Hendry said, sitting back. "What is it, Bev? You look more put out than usual."

Bev wished she could tell Hendry everything, though she had a feeling the empath-powered mayor already knew what was going on in her town.

"There's a lot of disruption in Pigsend right now," Bev said. "Not just the festival, but the judges. Warford looked like he was going to have me arrested for not being quick enough with the new judge's room."

"Bombadom," Hendry sat back. "Stoic fellow. Gives me the creeps." She pointed at Bev with her quill. "Don't you dare share that."

"What are we going to do about Dane and Rustin?" Bev asked.

"Not a thing," Hendry said. "You've got my permission to sit this one out. Let the events unfold without you meddling in them."

"Didn't you tell me—"

"I told you to set your dog on it," Hendry said. "You said he didn't find anything, right?"

"Right, but—"

"I know," Hendry replied with an honest smile. "You've got too good a heart, Bev. Even if the sinkhole hadn't appeared at your front door, I have a feeling you'd have ended up solving it for us the way you did, if only to protect this town that you love so much."

"Yes, but I'd prefer it if it wasn't someone staying at my inn..." Bev stopped. "Do you think Karolina's arresting people? Maybe that's why she doesn't want to look into their disappearances. Or maybe Warford and Bombadom are sending her to do their dirty work."

"Why would she want Rustin arrested? Or Dane, for that matter?" Hendry said. "And while our two Harvest Festival judges aren't my favorite individuals, I think their bark is worse than their bite. They're going to shut down people left and right, but I doubt they're going to have people arrested. Even if they were, they wouldn't do it in the dead of night. The queen's people like a *spectacle*."

Bev wasn't sure about that. "But—"

"Sit it out, Bev," Hendry said. "Goodness knows you have enough on your plate. Shouldn't you be testing new bread recipes?"

Chapter Nine

Hendry's guidance to *sit this one out* was eerily similar to what Andres had told her about the cursing. Bev had taken great offense to the idea that her meddling was anything other than her desire to find the truth. She returned to the inn, checking on her chickens and popping the three loaves of bread into the oven. Within minutes, the scent of rosemary wafted through the kitchen, and for once, it didn't fill Bev with happiness. Rather, it was an unpleasant reminder of Warford's disdain, and that Bev needed to figure something else out if she wanted to win first place.

It was silly, especially in light of the missing people, but it was something to distract her, as spinning her wheel wouldn't accomplish anything. She didn't have a recipe she followed for her famous Weary Dragon Inn rosemary bread, just dough from the night before, rosemary, more flour, salt, and water. The bread came together by feel, and it had taken her nearly a year of daily breadmaking with Wim to be able to know instinctively when it was ready. She'd tweaked her process, of course, especially with a longer proofing in the cold root cellar, but the ingredients—and rosemary—were always the same.

She could, of course, just submit her bread without any rosemary, but that seemed…well, dull. It would be fine, a delicious loaf to be sure, but award-winning? For that, she'd have to dig into Wim's recipe box.

Unfortunately, there wasn't another bread recipe to be found. Other than the delicious dinners Bev cooked, there were crisps, scones, pies, even a cake, though Bev had never used it. She went through the cards a few times, checking to make sure none of them had stuck together.

"Now, I remember there being another bread recipe," Bev said to Biscuit, who was interested in the oven. "Maybe it's in Wim's old things."

Biscuit sniffed.

"Come on, it's up in the attic."

She headed to the second floor, finding the trapdoor to the attic at the very end of the hallway.

Using a broomstick to catch the string, she pulled gently, revealing a wooden ladder and a dark, musty space. With her glowing stick illuminating her path, she once again remembered she needed to get up here and clean.

"When I have a minute," she replied, chuckling. She'd said that last year, too.

After a bit of searching, she found what she was looking for: Wim's old chest that she'd stashed up here when he died. She couldn't bear to get rid of it, and even now, as she carefully opened the top, she found herself misty-eyed as she peered down on his most treasured items. There wasn't much, of course. His white shirts, his dark pants. His boots, which were always clean. She shuffled around, looking for anything that looked like his recipe cards.

Instead, she pulled out a journal, something she'd forgotten about completely. Wim would jot down his thoughts about the day—observations, especially when it came to the management of the inn or his delicious meals. Bev hadn't felt right about peering inside immediately after his death, but now, enough time had passed that it seemed okay.

"Sorry, Wim," Bev said to the open air as she untied the leather wrap around it.

To her surprise, what she unwrapped wasn't a journal at all.

Wim McKee's Guide To
Running and Managing
The Weary Dragon Inn

"Well, this might've been good to have several years ago," Bev said with a chuckle. She sat more comfortably on the ground, stuffing the glowing stick in the open chest so she could read the journal. In a classic Wim move, the first page was dedicated to the schedule—the very same one Bev had stuck to these past six years. Up at dawn, feed Sin and check the root cellar. Start the day's bread. Finish scrubbing dishes and clean the kitchen. Say hello to the guests and see them off, then start their laundry. It was comforting to see how well she'd stuck to his tutelage, though she knew nothing else and wasn't the sort of person to try something new—except when it came to bread.

She flipped the pages, finding some recipes that matched the cards down in her kitchen, talking about what to do with rowdy customers, the recipe for the beer Bev served. Not much seemed to be new, though having it all in one neat bundle would've been quite helpful when Bev was having to outsource the management of the inn to Allen during the Lower Pigsend debacle.

She kept flipping through until she spotted something that looked promising. At the end of one of the long recipes for a rib roast was a short recipe for dinner rolls. Wim's note indicated they were delicious but entirely too time-consuming to make for the benefit of the inn on a regular basis. The measurements seemed close enough to her rosemary bread recipe, except she'd use milk and butter instead of water and add a little sugar.

"I think this'll do," Bev said.

With a smile, she closed Wim's crate and patted it a few times. She wasn't one for nostalgia or getting emotional, but she did owe...well, everything to the taciturn owner of the Weary Dragon. He'd let her stay, even though he hadn't needed her help, and given her a purpose and place in the world when she didn't know anything about herself.

"I hope I've done you proud," she whispered, wiping away a tear. "And I hope you aren't too mad at me for entering the Harvest Festival."

She left the attic, dusting off her shirt and closing the door behind her. Biscuit had been waiting patiently and followed her down the stairs as she pondered the timing of her new project. She could get the ingredients together tonight, do her bulk proofing overnight then get everything shaped and ready for the morning and a test run. She didn't want to submit something without trying it first.

With that plan, she pulled out all her ingredients. The recipe called for her to melt some butter and sugar in milk over the stove, so she started with that then let the mixture cool until it was just warm to the touch. She poured that in her bowl with the dough from the night before, plus enough flour to get the mixture to come together in a similar texture to her bread, as Wim had written.

She put that aside and washed her hands, checking on the bread and chicken in the oven, then peering out to the front room to see if anyone had come back yet. She had some time, so she tidied and straightened the front room, wiping the tables again, even though they were already clean. She thought about what Hans had said regarding the queen's people demanding licensure from every industry and coming to shut down the inn because she didn't follow proper protocol. She chuckled to herself, thinking about Warford inspecting her tables for dust.

Then she sobered because the judge might *just* do that.

She checked the time then returned to the kitchen to start her first round of kneading. Wim's recipe called for stretching the dough every thirty minutes until she'd done that four times.

"Well, you aren't too bad," she said, after finishing the last of the stretches. "Suppose you'll sit for a bit. Maybe by the end of dinner, you'll be ready to shape into rolls."

It was getting close to dinner, so Bev pulled everything out for it to cool a bit before she plated up. Already the front room sounded like it was crowded, and she hoped she might see a bigger group than the previous nights, if only to confirm to herself that things were getting back to normal. When she stepped out with the first round of platters, she counted only a half-full room once again.

"Dinner is served," she announced, forcing a smile.

There was a mix of people—many faces Bev hadn't ever seen before, presumably festivalgoers looking to fill up before making the trek back home, but also some vendors and a few locals. And, of course, the usual set of Earl, Etheldra, Max, and Bardoff.

"Finally caught up with the boys," Bardoff said. "Well, PJ at least. Not sure where Grant's run off to, but..."

"Dane Sterling's gone missing," Bev said. "He's pretty upset about it."

"I'm sure you've informed our *wonderful* interim sheriff," Etheldra said with a look. "And I'm *sure* she's taking it seriously."

"She's been informed," Bev said, glancing at the others in line and deciding to leave it at that. The last thing she wanted was to set the rumor mill going with her saying disparaging things about Her Majesty's chosen representative.

"Ms. Hunter's quite busy," Bardoff, ever the

queen apologist, piped up from behind Etheldra. "Her Majesty's arrival should be any day now, you know. I'm sure there's lots for Ms. Hunter to do to prepare."

"The festival's half over," Etheldra said. "*Her Majesty* might as well just skip it at this rate."

"Oh, I'm sure she'll be here tomorrow," Bardoff said. "Being the queen, she must have a lot of demands on her time. She probably got waylaid by some important business."

Etheldra surveyed him with a raised brow. "Mm. Come, Earl. Let's find a spot."

Bev was grateful Etheldra kept her opinions to herself, as she didn't want to have to break up an argument. Bardoff, for once, looked a little less enthusiastic about Her Majesty as he piled things onto his plate.

"It is a bit…well, I'm not saying… erm… A lot of us have been making preparations," he said. "I know things happen, but trying to get an answer out of Ms. Hunter is like pulling teeth."

"I know," Bev said. "And I'm sorry you and the children are left hanging until you know for sure."

He paused. "*Do* you think something's happened to Dane? The same thing that happened to Rustin? Goodness, I hope it's not another spate of events like those cursings. Bernard was never caught. Maybe he's back to terrorize the town."

"I don't think Bernard's back," Bev said. "It's

possible Dane left on a trip and forgot to tell Grant about it."

That seemed to hearten Bardoff, but Bev didn't quite believe that. For one, Dane wasn't the sort to do that, and for another, the missing items in his attic were curious enough to give her pause—and that was enough of a pattern that it linked him to Rustin. But they were two very different men, and other than a similar scene, she couldn't find a link between them.

The line moved, and Bev said her hellos to the vendors she'd met the previous few nights, as well as the new faces in the crowd. Many folks said they hailed from Middleburg and were eager to taste the famous Weary Dragon Inn rosemary bread. Bev was happy to see that they, at least, enjoyed it, even if the Harvest Festival judges didn't.

She popped back into the kitchen a few times to check on the rolls, which were growing a lot faster than she'd anticipated, but still weren't ready for the oven. When she came back out to the front room, the conversation had stopped completely. Warford and Bombadom had arrived, none of them looking happy to be there. Bev wiped her hands and forced a smile as she walked to her spot.

"Welcome," she said, gesturing to the table. "There's plenty of food."

She half-expected them to declare someone under arrest, but instead, they took the last of the plates and served themselves. It was hard to ignore the way the rest of the crowd glowered at them, but Bev tried her best.

"Is everything in the room to your liking, Mr. Bombadom?" Bev asked.

The stoic judge nodded once.

"Glad to hear it," Bev said. "We've got the livestock contest tomorrow, don't we?"

"Yes, indeed," Warford said. "And I anticipate it being a hotbed of problems, as the rest of the festival has been."

"I can't imagine why," Bev said. "Is there some kind of licensure for raising cattle, too?"

Warford sniffed at her, clearly not finding her joke funny. "There's a *severe* lack of administrative oversight in this town. I hear there was some kerfuffle with the apothecary recently, something about him *cursing* people? Karolina said he gave her the slip, but I know Her Majesty's people are scouring the countryside for him."

They would certainly *be* scouring for some time. "That was just a one-off," Bev said.

"I've also been informed there have been buildings collapsing out of nowhere, a wedding that was cursed, and giant chickens terrorizing the town during a magical storm," Bombadom said, his gaze boring a hole into Bev. "That certainly sounds like a pattern."

"Well, it was a good thing Zed Mackey was here

when that magical storm happened," Bev said. "And everything went back to normal quickly."

"I don't think you understand, Ms. Bev," Bombadom continued. "Her Majesty's impending arrival necessitates the correcting of all the maladies in town."

"And what, exactly, needs correcting?" Etheldra asked. "I heard you interrogating my business partner earlier today. I've been running my tea shop exactly the same way for almost fifty years. I daresay it's just fine—"

"Just because something's been run the same way doesn't mean it can't be improved upon," Bombadom said. "Especially when it comes to Her Majesty."

"Well, I think that's enough," Bev said, interjecting before Etheldra said something that would get her arrested. "Please, I'm sure it's been a long day. You two sit and enjoy your meal."

"Mm." Bombadom gave her a once-over and said nothing as he took his plate to the now-empty table, Warford right on his heels. Everyone else who'd been eating had lost their appetite and quickly brought their plates and bowls to Bev. She half-heartedly wished she could join them in their hasty escape, but unfortunately, the only place she could go to was the kitchen. There were dishes to wash, and when she checked her rolls, they were ready for the oven.

"Who doesn't love eating dinner rolls at midnight?" Bev said with a sigh as she went to add more logs to the oven fire. There were still ashes smoldering from dinner, but if she didn't cook these tonight, they'd be a goopy mess by morning.

Still, as she glanced at the clock, she mused that the rolls would be more or less on the same schedule as the rosemary bread. She'd have to get up a little earlier on the day of the final contest to get them going, but, assuming they tasted all right, they'd be a strong contender for first place.

"Well, unless Mr. Warford has an issue with rolls," Bev said. "I don't think there was anything in the rules about the shape, you know?"

Biscuit sniffed, his upper lip curling under and revealing a long tooth.

"You're right. Better check." She turned on her heel and walked out to where Warford and Bombadom were still eating—or rather, just Mr. Warford.

"Mr. Bombadom finish already?" Bev asked, collecting the plate. "That was fast."

"He had important business to attend to," Warford said.

"He's an interesting fellow," Bev said. "How long has he been in the judging corps?"

"He's not a member of Her Majesty's judging corps."

Bev stopped, turning to him. "Really?"

"Her Majesty's impending arrival and all the problems I found in Pigsend necessitated a different sort of inspection," Warford said, rising and handing her his empty plate. "Rest assured, Duke Bombadom will scour every inch of this town to ensure it's proper for Her Majesty's arrival."

Bev took his plate and forced a neutral smile. "Well, aren't we lucky, then? I'm sure he'll do a wonderful job." She cleared her throat. "I did have a question about the bread-making contest. A rule clarification," she added quickly when he glared at her.

"Yes?"

"Is there any rule against rolls?" Bev asked. "Dinner rolls, specifically."

He rubbed his chin thoughtfully. "I don't *believe* so. They're made with the same ingredients as your other bread?"

"Some slight modifications," Bev said. "But otherwise, yes."

"I will check the rulebook, but to my knowledge, that should be fine."

Bev thanked him and hastily returned to the kitchen, reeling from his words and wondering what they meant, and almost missed the small piece of paper sitting on her kitchen table. When she picked it up, magic buzzed on her fingertips, and when she read the words, her stomach sank.

Would you mind coming to visit soon? Shamus has gone missing, and I'm worried about him.

- P

Chapter Ten

Percival, the wizard who kept Lower Pigsend running, had never summoned Bev like this, and Shamus being added to the list of those missing was a new wrinkle in the concerning pattern Bev had been seeing. She had, up until now, avoided going to Merv's since she'd discovered the reason behind the cursing. With Karolina in town, it just seemed too dangerous to even head that way. But she couldn't ignore this note, which erupted into purple flames as soon as she finished reading it.

The good news was most of the town would be up north for the livestock judging in the morning, including Mr. Warford and *Duke* Bombadom. Bev hadn't a clue about the hierarchies in Her Majesty's court, but *duke* sounded quite high. Coupled with his already concerning interest in the tea shop and his comment about correcting things, the citizens of Pigsend had perhaps only seen the start of his meddling.

In the morning, after finishing her chores, Bev packed the dinner rolls she'd baked the night before into her basket. Merv would certainly enjoy them, and thanks to Warford and Bombadom leaving without saying a word to Bev, she was able to stuff a few blueberry muffins as well.

"Watch the inn, will you, Biscuit?" Bev said as she prepared to leave.

The laelaps promptly went to sleep in front of the hearth.

Basket in hand, Bev took the long way out of town, just to avoid being seen by anyone. She'd stop every few minutes to make sure no one was following her, then continued. By the time she was past most of the farms, she relaxed, as the hills and wide-open spaces would make it difficult for someone to follow without her noticing.

Still, she scanned the countryside for a few extra minutes before ducking through the dark tunnel down toward Merv's house. At the end, Bev rapped a few times on the familiar orange door and waited, admiring the green shutters and the woven mat, which looked new. Merv, a six-foot moleman, had first met Bev during the sinkhole fiasco, and in the months since had become a dear friend, always interested in the latest curiosities happening in town. Besides being a knitting aficionado, he was also somewhat well-versed what was possible with magic, though once Bev became acquainted with Percival, an actual wizard, Merv's role had been reduced to the provider of the meeting space and tea.

"Coming, coming!" Merv's voice called from the other side. The door swung open, and Merv let out a cheer. "Goodness! It's been ages since I've seen you. Is everything all right up in Pigsend? Lillie hasn't been by in weeks!"

"Yes and no," Bev said with a smile. "I have a lot to catch you up on."

"I'll put on a kettle."

While Merv waddled to the kitchen, Bev sat on the couch and gave him the full story of what had been going on, from telling him the resolution of the cursing episode and Karolina Hunter's appearance in town, all the way to the Harvest Festival and the guest that should've been making her appearance any day now.

"The *queen*?" Merv said with a gasp. "In Pigsend? For the Harvest Festival?"

"I know. It makes very little sense," Bev said. "And so far, she hasn't arrived. But goodness, the town has been preparing nonstop anyway."

"So Lillie hasn't come with goodies because…?"

Merv asked, bringing out the kettle with two cups.

"Because like me, she's worried about Karolina or one of the other members of the queen's forces following her, especially with these new judges in town," Bev said. "And yes, I know Percival's spell is in effect, but the risk is just too high."

Bev glanced at the door on the other side of the room, the one that led to Lower Pigsend. Percival's charm on Merv's living room made said door invisible to members of the queen's forces (and Lillie, but that was a recent update), but it still made Bev uneasy.

"Not sure I agree with *that*, but..." Merv muttered, settling down with his cup and pulling the basket into his lap. "Why did you decide to visit now, if things aren't quite right yet?"

"I got a letter from Percival last night," Bev said. "He said Shamus was missing."

"He is?" Merv tutted, spearing a blueberry muffin with one of his long claws and popping it into his mouth. "Are you sure he's not gotten tired of being Percival's assistant? That's certainly what the Lower Pigsend scuttlebutt would have you believe..."

"Yes, except..." Bev told him about Rustin and Dane's disappearances. "There's no evidence, and I can't see a connection between the three of them, other than that Andres wanted Rustin fired, and Andres worked with Shamus—"

"He did?"

"Oh, right, I left that bit out," Bev said. "Shamus provided Andres with the recipe to make the potion used to cast the curses. In return, Shamus saved Bernard from Karolina." She snapped her fingers, looking at the door. "You know, it might be a good time to pop down and see *him*, too."

"Bernard? I heard about him," Merv said with an emphatic nod. "He's the new, hot thing down in Lower Pigsend. Everyone's so excited to have a *real* apothecary. I daresay he's taken quite the load off Percival."

"Come now, Gerry is an apothecary," Bev said.

Merv made a noise. "Hardly. I avoided buying anything from him if I could."

"He's still down there, isn't he?" Bev said. "Gerry. Is he getting along with his brother? Still a chicken?"

"I'm not sure. I… Oh, what is *this?*" He'd gone through the muffins and found the dinner rolls stashed beneath. "A new bread recipe?"

"One of those lovely Harvest Festival judges doesn't like rosemary, apparently," Bev said.

"How rude." He popped the roll into his mouth and made a joyful noise. "Bev, these are delightful!"

"Are they?" Bev said. "They're a bit cold. I had to bake them last night while I was figuring out the timing. They're involved to make, too. Parsing out each individual roll takes a while, and I'm not sure

Warford's going to let me enter them."

"Well, he *must*. They're bread—just in a different shape. I don't think he'd find fault with that."

"You'd be surprised," Bev muttered, glancing at the clock. "You know, I probably should be heading down to Percival's so I can get back before the crowd returns to Pigsend. I don't want anyone to question where I went."

"I'm happy to entertain any queen's soldier who walks through my door."

"I would rather we avoid it," Bev said with a wave of her hand as she rose. "Is there anything I can bring to Lower Pigsend for you?"

"Oh, you're a dear, but no. I've got three blankets to finish up today, then I'll bring them down myself. Doing quite the brisk business lately."

Bev smiled. "I'm glad. Nice to keep busy, isn't it?"

"Not as if you ever get a day of rest." Merv chuckled. "Though I suppose winter will be arriving soon up there. Maybe a chance to slack off a bit."

"Hope springs eternal."

~

Bev left Merv to polish off the basket of dinner rolls and walked through the door to Lower Pigsend. The tunnel seemed longer than usual, perhaps because Bev was feeling the clock. When she stepped out of the darkness and into the dim light of the town, she strolled down the busy street, debating her first stop. She did need to see Percival, but the conversation about Bernard had made her curious. Andres had said—and Vellora had reiterated—that Bernard was content in his new home, and that Bev shouldn't be angry with them for the abrupt transition. She wanted to see for herself, so she could put that concern to rest.

But as she rounded the corner to the apothecary, she stopped, gaping. Gerry's shop had been completely transformed. The footprint had been doubled—at least—plus there was an entire second story on top. A line to get inside wound around the corner, and as Bev approached the window, she found the spacious interior also crammed to the gills with people.

"Goodness," Bev muttered, putting her hand over her eyes to peer inside. She couldn't even see the counter, let alone Bernard or Gerry.

"Oy!" A very annoyed-looking, tall creature with what appeared to be tree bark for skin was glaring at her. "Get in line! Some of us have been waiting all day."

"Oh, I'm not here for a tincture," Bev said, holding up her hands in defense. "I just wanted—"

But the chorus of angry voices demanding she wait her turn sent her scurrying across the street. The front door opened, and a small, pink-winged creature fluttered out carrying a vial nearly the same size as she was. The bark-skinned man pushed his way inside, but he only got halfway through the door. The entire queue shifted up one person then resumed its waiting.

"Clearly, not getting in there," Bev muttered, looking around. One of the members of the queue was glaring at her, perhaps sensing that she was still trying to cut the line (despite her just wanting a chat, not a tincture), so Bev turned on her heel and walked the other way.

She wasn't quite ready to give up, so she did a large loop around the block, then came to the back of the shop. There wasn't a door or anything that would get her inside, which seemed odd. Why would there only be a single door at the front? She gazed up and down and around, but didn't—

Before her eyes, the bricks that made up the back wall of the shop twisted in on themselves, pulling back until they revealed a tall man carrying a large bag and looking disgruntled. He stepped out into the alley, turning as the bricks reassembled themselves back into a wall, and started to leave when he noticed Bev gawking at him.

She didn't recognize him, but he certainly did her. "*You.*"

"Me?" Bev looked around. "I don't..." It took her a moment, but the voice sparked her memory. "Gerry?"

Bernard's brother, fully human and without the

yellow feathers, beak, and chicken legs Bev was used to seeing on him, glared at her as if she'd done something to personally offend him. Not as if they'd ever gotten on well, but Bev was a bit taken aback by the degree of his disgust toward her.

"H-Hi," Bev said, catching herself after a moment. "I see you're all, um…cured?"

Gerry snorted, glaring at his former shop. "Yes, isn't it just *wonderful*? Bernie arrived in town a few weeks ago. Something about almost being arrested for magic, I'm not *sure* of the specifics. But Shamus told me to move over, welcome him into my own store, give him space to set up. Next thing I know…" He gestured to the store, and presumably, the line that hadn't been there when he'd been the only apothecary in town. "Everyone's just *so happy*."

"Clearly not everyone," Bev muttered. "But you're no longer feathery, so that's good, isn't it?"

"Is it?" He scowled. "Reduced to being an errand boy in my own shop. Haven't made a potion in *weeks*. But can I leave? No. Gotta stay and help my *dear brother*." He gestured to the bag hanging from his arm. "Suppose he's still got to keep his above ground clients happy, too. This particular bag is going to *Nog*."

Bev hoped Nog wasn't making deliveries at the moment, but she'd be sure to mention it to Percival when she saw him.

"Erm, I do hate to be a bother, but," Bev smiled,

"would it be possible for me to say hello to Bernard? I know he's probably busy, but—"

Gerry rolled his eyes, an act that took twice as long as it should've and came with a whole-body sigh, then turned to the bricks, which also seemed annoyed to be bothered again. But they pulled back, revealing the back of the apothecary shop.

"Go right ahead. I'm sure he'll be *happy* to see you." He shouldered the bag. "I've got to make deliveries. Toodle-oo."

Bev watched him leave, getting the sense that he was in no hurry to complete his task, then headed into the dark room. As soon as she stepped beyond the bricks, they hastily reconfigured themselves again, and Bev had to hope they'd be kind enough to let her out. She doubted the crowd in the front room would be amenable, especially that bark-skinned fellow.

The room itself was lined with shelves bearing tins, vials, vases, and even a few large jugs sitting on the ground. Magic tingled on Bev's skin, as if everything in this room was infused with it. Bernard's shop back in Pigsend had had quite the plethora of ingredients on shelves, too, but the longer Bev walked the length of the room, the bigger it seemed to get.

"Erm, Bernard?" she called, remembering she was on something of a timetable. "Are you back here?"

"Around the corner!"

Bev followed the sound of his voice and found the former Pigsend apothecary standing at a table with several glass vials of varying sizes. A small purple flame held a bubbling, circular glass jar aloft, and bags floated around the room—some sparkled with blue sparks, while others had something writhing inside. The magic that had settled on Bev's skin increased, and she rubbed the goosebumps down on her arms.

"Yes? Can I—" Bernard spun, wearing a pair of goggles that made his eyes look three times the size they were supposed to be. "Bev?" He pulled off the goggles, and his eyes went back to normal. "Is it really you?"

"Hi, Bernard," Bev said, walking forward with her hand outstretched.

"Oh, aren't you a sight for sore eyes?" He took her hand and squeezed it. "I'm so happy to see you! What in the world are you doing down here?"

"It's…a long story," Bev said. "But I'm here to check on you. Are you all right? I'm so sorry about what happened with Karolina and—"

"Blessing in disguise!" He gestured to the shop then stopped. "Oh, that's *right*, you'd said you'd seen my brother. I bet you've been down here a bunch, haven't you?"

"As I said, it's—" Bev stopped speaking as one of the writhing bags floated by her face.

"Shoo!" Bernard said, waving it away. "Sorry about that. Sometimes these ingredients get a little hard to handle. Come, come. I'm positively swamped with orders, but I'm happy to chat while I work."

"So you're…okay?" Bev said, following him back to the table. "Being down here? With Gerry—"

"It was a shock at first, I won't lie. One minute, I'm standing at the Weary Dragon, about to be arrested by Karolina Hunter. The next, the whole world slows down, and a wizard named Shamus appears, telling me he's got a place for me if I'm willing to come start a new apothecary business in his town." He chuckled. "I told him if it's a choice between him and going in irons with Karolina, I'll take the wizard."

"Probably a good idea," Bev said. "Did he mention—"

"So I show up here, in this amazing town just down the road from Pigsend, and who do I see standing in the apothecary shop but my dear brother Gerry!" He let out a sigh. "Well, the old codger looked exactly the same as I remembered him, but goodness, it was good to see him. I'd been carrying around that vial to turn him human, so of course, I handed that over immediately and *poof*, he was back to the brother I'd grown up with." He chuckled. "A few more wrinkles and gray hair, but basically the same."

Bev nodded. "And you two started working together?"

"It's been a busy few weeks. Of course, I started by working with him, but..." He made a face. "Well, my brother's skill hasn't improved quite as much as one would've hoped, so the customers started asking for my potions. Then the lines came, and now I'm busier than I've ever been. We had to hire three people out front just to take orders!" He gestured toward the ceiling. "Plus, I've still got Winston delivering to my upstairs clients."

"All of them?" Bev asked. "Even the ones who were...?"

"Well, not them." Bernard sighed. "I hear I've become the scapegoat for whatever was going on up there, so I haven't heard much from the folks I cured. But that's all right. The truth will come out eventually. But until then, it's been wonderful to be here and doing what I love without having to worry about Karolina looking over my shoulder."

Bev watched him, conflicted. She could tell him about Andres's plan, and how he was the unfortunate patsy who'd taken the fall so Rustin could be fired. And it might not faze him that much, especially with as busy and happy as he was. But it was precisely *because* he looked so happy—happier than he had even living in Pigsend—that Bev let it alone.

"Well, I know you're busy," she said, taking his

hand. "I just wanted to pop in on my way to chat with Percival."

"You *do* know more than you let on, don't you, Bev?" Bernard said.

Bev smiled. "Sometimes. Take it easy, Bernard."

Chapter Eleven

"Bev, thank you so much for coming," Percival said, rushing forward to squeeze her hands.

Bev had headed straight to the Merchant's House after speaking with Bernard, eager to get on with her day. She still felt…uneasy about Bernard's current situation but could at least sleep better knowing he was truly happy. When she'd arrived, she'd found Percival's line much shorter than usual, though without the wizard's apprentice to direct traffic, there was more of a gaggle than a line. As she approached, Percival appeared to wave her back quickly, much to the annoyance of all who'd gathered.

"Of course," Bev said. "We have a lot to discuss.

What happened with Shamus?"

"Well, I'm not sure," he said, sitting on his purple chair. Candles floated around the room, like the bags of ingredients at Bernard's, but by now, Bev was used to them and gratefully sat on the chair Percival conjured for her. "We hadn't had any sort of argument or row, at least not in a few weeks—"

"Was the last one about Bernard?" Bev asked.

He shook his head. "Why would it be about Bernard?"

"He didn't tell you how you ended up with such a wonderful apothecary, who happens to be Gerry's brother?" Bev asked. When Percival said he hadn't a clue, Bev filled him in, and the old wizard's frown grew more and more pronounced.

"I'm not sure what makes me angrier," he said, after she'd finished. "His role in the subterfuge, the fact that he cast such *advanced* magic in front of Her Majesty's soldiers, or that he lied to me about the entire incident."

"Lied to Bernard as well," Bev said. "I was just at his shop, checking up on him. He seems…happy. Gerry's back to being human."

"And we do have a highly skilled apothecary able to keep up with demand," Percival said. "My workload's been cut in half."

"He's that good?" Bev said.

Percival nodded. "But the way Shamus went about it… I don't like any of it. Unfortunately, now he's missing, so I can't have a discussion with him about his reckless behavior, can I?"

"When was the last time you saw him?" Bev asked. "Was there anything strange or different about him?"

"No, it was a normal day. We don't talk much when there's a line, so if there was something amiss, he didn't mention it. His last task of the evening was to head up to the surface to meet with Winston for a hand-off of Bernard's tinctures. I don't even know if that happened or if…" He tutted. "Well, I haven't seen one of Her Majesty's soldiers walking down the street, so I assume he wasn't taken prisoner with the door open."

"I might've heard about that," Bev said. "But there have also been a few curious missing folks in Pigsend. One slightly connected to Shamus, too. Andres, the one who'd planned Bernard's framing, did it to get Sheriff Rustin fired. Then Rustin disappeared on the first day of the Harvest Festival."

"Hm." Percival tapped his chin.

"More interesting is his house looks like someone ransacked it searching for something, digging a hole in the kitchen, and Biscuit scented something magical in the dirt," she continued. "That house was built for Rustin, so I don't know if someone buried something before it was constructed then returned to Pigsend to dig it up."

"And the other missing person?" Percival asked.

"Dane Sterling. Farmer. He *also* had something slightly magical in his attic that was missing. But he's not..." She sighed. "There's not really a connection between him and the other two. Even the one connecting Rustin and Shamus is tenuous at best."

"Indeed." He sat back. "You said the Harvest Festival was ongoing?"

She nodded. "And get this—Queen Meandra is supposed to be paying us a visit."

Percival stood up so quickly he knocked over his chair. "The *queen* is coming? Goodness, why didn't you lead with that?"

Bev frowned. "I—Oh, I'm sorry, I—"

Percival began pacing around the room. "I've got to strengthen all our charms. I need to cast an extra protective spell around the town just to ensure... It's such a good thing Bernard is here, because otherwise I might not have the strength... Yes, I should see if he can help me with a protective potion, too. I—" He stopped, noticing Bev. "I do apologize, Bev, but you do have to go."

Before Bev could say another word, a haze of magic washed over her, and when she came to, she was back in Merv's living room, mind still buzzing from the conversation with Percival. Her gaze immediately swept to the door to Lower Pigsend, which faded from her view in seconds.

"B-Bev!" Merv hopped upright, dropping his

basket of yarn. "Where did you come from?"

"Percival said he needed me out of Lower Pigsend," Bev said. "Strengthening his spells since the queen's on her way."

"I see." Merv followed her gaze to the missing door and sighed. "Well, there go my plans to sell these blankets tomorrow. I'll just have to hang onto them until the queen leaves town." He chortled. "Suppose that means you and Lillie won't be shy about coming to visit, eh? Those blueberry muffins were fine, but not quite the deliciousness I expect from you lot now. Can't say I blame myself. I've been spoiled."

Bev smiled, but her attention was still on the door.

"Did Percival tell you what happened to Shamus?"

"Seems like it's unimportant now," Bev said. "If Shamus decided to disappear for a bit, I don't think he'll find his way back into Lower Pigsend anytime soon."

"Well, that's less work for you, then," Merv said. "You can spend more time on those delicious rolls. I'm sure they'll win first place this year."

The clock on the wall chimed, and Bev shook her head. "Must be getting back. I don't doubt Percival's charms are potent, but I'd rather not be blamed for a queen's soldier sniffing around your living room." She smiled at him. "I think this might be goodbye for a while."

"Well, that sounds positively awful," Merv said. "I don't think I should be punished because some silly soldiers are here. Percival's charm is quite good, and I'm sure even if they came to my front door—"

Bev held up her hands. "I don't want to risk it. Besides, these two judges seem to have it out for everyone. I daresay they'd find fault with a moleman such as yourself. Even as lovely as you are."

He snorted. "Well, if it gets too dangerous for Lillie, do tell her she can stay here until they leave."

"That's very generous of you," Bev said.

"Generous of me? I'd get a pobyd living in my midst," he said with a chuckle. "Be sure to send her with plenty of flour and sugar, too. And fruit! Oh, some more of those blueberry muffins would be exquisite. Just with magic, this time. And a sugary icing. Lemon, too. Delicious. I know she's got a recipe like that."

Bev smiled. "If it gets to that point, I'll let her know. But my fervent hope is that we get through the next few days of the festival without any more surprises."

Merv rose and walked over, holding out his large, furry arms. "Be safe, Bev. You never know when *you* might just run afoul of these soldiers."

Bev thought of Bombadom and cringed. "Let's hope not."

Bev left shortly after hugging her dear friend and

promising she'd return as soon as it was safe. Merv had always had a laid-back approach when it came to Lower Pigsend, which had, unfortunately, landed him in a bit of hot water when Lillie had stolen the talisman.

The light from the surface shone at the top of the tunnel, and Bev quickened her pace, thinking about all she'd have to do when she got back to the inn. But she stopped short when a figure stood in front of the tunnel, blocking most of the sun.

Bev swallowed—had someone followed her after all?

But as she drew closer, she recognized the broad shoulders and lack of hair, and completely relaxed when a low voice called out, "Hi, Bev."

"Andres!" Bev exclaimed, nearly tripping over her feet as she rushed up the tunnel.

Vellora's commander met her halfway, wearing a kind smile that showed nothing of his underhanded dealings and big plans.

"I figured this was the safest place," he said. "Though I couldn't help but feel quite a shift just now. Did something happen down in Lower Pigsend?"

"Percival's been made aware of Her Majesty's impending arrival," Bev said. "And took extra precautions."

"For the best," Andres said, surprising Bev a little. "There are lots of folks who'd be *very* eager to find out about the doorway to that lovely little village."

"Which is why I wanted to chat," Bev said. "Percival told me Shamus is missing."

Andres's brows shot up. "Shamus? Missing? For how long?"

"A few days, I think. Percival was quick to shoo me out of Lower Pigsend when he found out about Her Majesty's arrival," Bev said. "Have you heard anything about that?"

"I haven't," Andres said. "But that's quite concerning. Thank you for telling me. A wizard like Shamus wouldn't just disappear like that, you know? Not without causing quite a stir."

Bev chewed her lip. "So you aren't…behind it?"

"Behind what? Shamus going missing?" He shook his head. "No."

"What about Rustin and Dane Sterling?" Bev asked.

"Rustin's missing, too?" he said. "And I'm not sure I'm acquainted with Dane Sterling."

"Andres, please don't lie—"

"I'm not, I swear on my loyalty to the kingside," he said, holding up his hands. "My only instruction was to ensure Rustin got fired. I don't know anything about Rustin or the other man going missing."

She opened her mouth then paused. "Instruction? You mean it wasn't your idea to get him fired?"

He shook his head. "I was given my orders."

"By whom?"

"Can't say," he said with a grin. "As to why those specific orders, I have my guesses, of course, but I don't know." He held up his hands again. "The truth as I know it."

She huffed, annoyed that there were somehow *more* layers of secrecy. "Why didn't you tell me about Rustin's firing being an *order* a few weeks ago? Why make me think it was all your idea?"

"My soldiers follow me because they think I'm in charge," he said. "Until such time that I'm willing to tell them otherwise, it's not necessary for them to know." He paused. "Are you sure they're missing and not just on holiday?"

"I wouldn't have thought anything of it, except Biscuit was interested in things in their house— things that had gone missing that contained traces of magic," Bev said. "And with Shamus now missing…"

"Who is Dane?" Andres asked.

"As far as I know, he's a farmer," Bev said. "He had a cousin who fought for the kingside, so the rumor said. But I'm not sure what Dane did during the war. Either way, there was a chest in his attic that had been recently disturbed, and his cousin's son, who was staying there, said it wasn't like him to not come back."

"I'll see what I can find out," Andres said. "But I don't think it's... Well, it's not unusual for farmers to leave home after they've finished their harvest, right? And as for Rustin, from what Vellora tells me, he took his firing quite hard, so maybe—"

"Firing that you orchestrated," Bev said with a glare.

He actually smiled at her. "You're still sore about that? Didn't you get a chance to speak with Bernard down there? He's thriving."

"Well, yes, but—"

"A small amount of pain for a larger gain," Andres said. "And speaking of that, while I know you're probably concerned about these missing folks, you might want to keep your head down and focus on innkeeping."

"Oh yeah?" Bev scowled. "Why? Would it interfere with your plans?"

"No plans to interfere with at the moment," he said. "But you have a very particular guest at your inn that merits extra caution. Duke Bombadom isn't just any judge. He's one of Meandra's favorite minions. Quite renowned in the kingside towns for his ruthlessness in sniffing out magic and magical nonsense and leaving the people absolutely wretched in his wake."

Bev had had a hunch that was the case, but having it confirmed made her even more uncomfortable. "He said he was in town to ensure everything was correct for Her Majesty's arrival."

"I don't doubt it."

"Are you…" She doubted he'd tell her, but it couldn't hurt to ask. "You aren't planning on *doing* something to the queen, are you?"

He smiled. "Now, why would I tell you that?"

Bev sighed. It was worth a try. "But will you tell me if you're planning on ruining our Harvest Festival? I'd like to prepare, if so."

He chuckled. "Your festival is safe from me, but it may not be safe from Bombadom and Warford. If you know anyone hiding magic, it might be time to give them one of those iron-infused crisps you're so famous for. And to let every business owner in town know they should be prepared to hand over whatever gold they've got lying around or face the consequences."

"I don't understand why they're doing this," Bev said. "They've already canceled the farmers' market because the farmers don't have the right paperwork and haven't paid the right amount of gold. Etheldra said they were in her shop yesterday, and it sounds like Bombadom might want to shut *her* down, too. Goodness knows Stella Brewer has her hands full at the apothecary shop. Why are they terrorizing us like this?"

He sighed. "Because that's what Her Majesty's people *do*, Bev. Every town that didn't swear immediate fealty to Meandra has gone through the same thing. It was bound to happen to Pigsend sooner or later."

"And the queen's fine with this?"

"She doesn't care, as long as her coffers are full," Andres said. "This is what I was trying to tell you earlier. You may think I'm causing all this pain, but it's nothing in comparison to what's coming. Mark my words: Bombadom's just getting started. And you may not recognize Pigsend when he's through with it."

~

Unnerved by Andres's impromptu appearance, Bev returned to town more slowly than she probably should have. The livestock contest was still going on, so the town square looked even more empty than usual. The missing vendors, including the farmers, were obvious now, and Bev could only hope everyone who'd traveled had found another festival to vend at. The temperatures would be dropping soon, and Bev had to assume festivals would stop happening everywhere. It would be a long season until spring.

Still, she let that worry go. It wasn't hers to carry, and she had plenty weighing on her. She wasn't surprised Andres had told her to butt out, but she was somewhat surprised she finally felt inclined to listen. Not because she didn't care, but because she was starting to get the impression there were things afoot that even her even-keeled optimism wouldn't be any match for. Andres had certainly painted a bleak picture about what Bombadom had done to other towns, and he certainly hadn't changed his spots in Pigsend.

She opened the front door to the inn and was greeted with a horrifying sight. Bombadom stood in a corner, hoisting a chair at a snarling, barking Biscuit, who had nearly every hair on his body standing up straight as he drooled spit and snapped at the air.

"What in the world is—" Bev began, but Bombadom was faster.

"That *mongrel* is a menace!" Bombadom cried, pointing at the dog. "He bit me!"

Chapter Twelve

Bev leaped into action and grabbed Biscuit by his midsection. He didn't seem to notice her, writhing and continuing to bark aggressively at the judge in the corner. Bev all but wrestled him back into the kitchen, offering apologies over his incessant barking, then slammed the door with her foot to keep the laelaps from going back for a second bite.

Biscuit jumped out of her arms and paced the floor, growling angrily at the door.

"Now that's *quite* enough, Biscuit," Bev said. "What in the world has gotten into you? You cannot attack guests like that, do you understand?"

But the laelaps didn't seem to hear her, his loud

barking echoing in Bev's ears unpleasantly.

"*Biscuit*," Bev snapped.

He still ignored her, so she grabbed him by his snout and made him look at her. His wild eyes seemed unfamiliar, almost, but softened to their usual expression after a moment. Then he whimpered and wagged his tail, licking her palm before his entire body relaxed.

"You gave me a fright there," she said, scratching his ears. "What's going on?"

It really wasn't much use. The laelaps was many things, but a speaker wasn't one of them. But Biscuit turned his attention back to the door and emitted another low growl.

"Yes, he's awful, but that doesn't give you the right to bite him," Bev said, rising and putting her hand to her chest. "He's worse than you know, too. Goodness, what are we going to do?"

Biscuit sniffed, and Bev could practically read his mind. *Evict Bombadom.*

"No, unfortunately," Bev said with a shake of her head. "I've got to keep him happy, else the town might suffer more than it already has." With a heavy heart, she walked to the door. "You've got to stay outside."

He whimpered.

"Not..." She lowered her voice and approached him again. "Not *forever*, just until he leaves. Okay? But keep a low profile. Something tells me he won't take a bite lying down." She scratched his ears. "The last thing I want is him looking too closely at you."

Biscuit licked her hand again.

"Now go on," Bev said, a lump forming in her chest. "And stay out of sight. It's warm tonight, and there's plenty in the compost pile, so you won't go hungry."

His ears drooping, Biscuit padded out of the yard. Bev's heart broke—he looked absolutely pitiful—but she held fast. Her guests' safety came first, and whatever had gotten into Biscuit wasn't something Bomabdum would forget anytime soon.

She waited until Biscuit had disappeared around the corner before closing the kitchen door and taking a deep breath. Every ounce of energy she had went into plastering a neutral smile on her face and swallowing all her angry tirades about *what* the perfidious duke might've done to provoke her normally sweet laelaps. When she was sure she could keep a straight face, she returned to the front room.

Bombadom was sitting in one of the two chairs, a rag on his hand as he rubbed ointment onto it. "Can't let something like this get infected. Nasty animal. Can't believe you'd have something like that *living* at your inn."

"I'm terribly sorry," Bev said. "I don't know what's gotten into him. He's never done that before."

"You can't trust dogs," Bombadom said with a

glare. "Especially filthy mutts like the one you have. Why was he allowed inside? Dogs reside *outside*."

Bev didn't really have a response she wanted to share. "I do apologize, wholeheartedly, for his actions. But perhaps if you could tell me what you were doing before he attacked, that might help me understand what might've triggered him."

"I wasn't *doing* anything," Bombadom said with a sneer. "He just attacked me out of nowhere."

"He usually stays in the kitchen," Bev said. "Were you…in the kitchen?"

Bombadom sniffed, and the small twitch on his face said that he *had*, in fact, been in the kitchen. Which was strange, because he was *supposed* to be at the livestock judging with Warford.

Good boy, Biscuit.

"Where is that monster, anyway? Is he lying in wait to attack me again?" Bombadom asked, perhaps sensing that Bev was going to continue her line of questioning about the kitchen. "I will be sure to inform Karolina Hunter there's a dangerous dog staying at the inn. She'll have no trouble dealing with it, I'm sure."

Bev's heart seized. "That's not necessary, I promise you."

"And I promise you that it is!" He rose, holding the wet rag to his hand. "Now I don't know if you're aware, but I've been given the authority to lay down the law in this town, and that *includes* inspecting each business for the appropriate paperwork. I've had my hands full with the rest of this unruly village up until now, but with this newest incident, I have no choice but to investigate *your* business practices."

"I'm sure you'll find them satisfactory," Bev said. "The Weary Dragon's been run the same way for almost a hundred and fifty years now."

"And does that running include the housing of a dangerous animal?" Bombadom asked.

"Well, no," Bev said. Wim probably wouldn't have let Biscuit stay, though he wasn't usually out solving magical mysteries either. "But Biscuit is—"

"Not going to be a problem, if I have any say in the matter," Bombadom said, marching toward the staircase. "As soon as I retrieve my weapon, in case that monster's waiting for me, I'm going to see to it that creature is taken care of. Consider yourself lucky I don't take you to task for allowing such a creature to cohabitate in your inn," he said, giving her a once-over. "And I would watch your tongue unless you'd like me to change my mind on *that* matter."

As soon as Bombadom went upstairs, Bev headed out to look for Biscuit. Merv had said his home would be open to Lillie, but he'd almost certainly let Biscuit stay there, provided Bev threatened the laelaps to within an inch of his life about eating Merv's knitted goods.

She walked quickly the way Biscuit had gone, knowing Bombadom would be equally quick to find Ms. Hunter. But Biscuit was nowhere to be found. She doubled back and searched her root cellar, Sin's stable (earning a very angry bray from the sleeping mule), her compost pile—even the thicket where one half of her magical amulet had been buried. There wasn't any sign of him, not even a strand of golden fur.

"Oh, Biscuit," Bev muttered, coming out of the thicket and putting her hand to her head. She wouldn't be able to rest until she found him, not with Bombadom's threats, but...he was quite intelligent. Perhaps he'd taken her advice to heart and headed for the hills until the festival blew over instead of waiting for her to retrieve him. It would be safer for him that way, but it still made Bev anxious not to know where he was.

She was walking back to the inn, heavy-hearted, when she spotted Grant and PJ walking up the opposite way, both holding bags. Neither one looked happy.

"My mom told me to head back to Sheepsburg," PJ said, by way of greeting. "She said there were too many soldiers walking around this morning. So I wanted to say goodbye before we left."

"That's good," Bev said, gazing around the backyard just in case.

"Good?" PJ frowned. "Did you not hear the part about the soldiers?"

"Hm?" She turned to them then realized what he'd said. "Oh, you said there were more soldiers in town than before?"

"Yeah. They've been doing patrols, it looks like. Mom's worried they're gonna start asking questions, especially with that Bombadom wandering around sniffing into places he shouldn't," PJ said.

Bev nodded, once again, scouring her yard for any sign of Biscuit.

"Bev?" PJ said, catching her gaze. "What're you looking for?"

Bev turned to him, shaking her head. "Biscuit attacked Duke Bombadom, so I sent him outside. Now Bombadom wants to involve Karolina, so I'm trying to find Biscuit to get him to safety."

"What was Bombadom doing?" PJ said. "Biscuit's never done anything like that, has he?"

"No," Bev said. "And I'm sure Bombadom deserved it, but that doesn't change the fact that he's out to get Biscuit, and I'd like to find my dog before someone else does."

"That monster," Grant said. "You know, just yesterday, my aunt Apolinary had to fork over, like, fifty gold coins just to stay open. And fill out a form that said she was able to sew clothes. Can you believe that?"

"Why don't you walk with us?" PJ offered. "We

were already planning to take the roundabout way out of town. Maybe we'll find Biscuit along the way."

Bev was grateful for the help, and extra eyes, as the more time wore on without seeing any sign of Biscuit, the more she worried. With the boys' help, they checked every root cellar, especially ones owned by known magical folks, thickets, front porches, back porches, even stables. They even looked in Rosie Kelooke's yard, but the only thing there were the demonic chickens, who clucked menacingly at the intruders. As they walked the town, the soldiers PJ had mentioned became more numerous, which looked even more odd because the crowd of festivalgoers was still up north. They luckily didn't give the two teens or Bev a second look, but she felt PJ's anxiety every time they crossed paths. Finally, having exhausted the search, the trio headed north along the road to Sheepsburg.

"Maybe he went to the dark forest," PJ said, rubbing the back of his head as the mass of trees loomed in the distance. "That seems the sort of place he might go."

"Maybe. Might pop up there after sundown," Bev said. "The last thing I need is one of these soldiers asking me why I'm going there."

"Really?" Grant sniffed. "Why? It's just a spooky place, right?"

"Spooky and magical," Bev said. "Which is the sort of place Biscuit might go, to be honest. He could hide himself quite well there."

She kept walking with them until the close-in farms were no more, and there was nothing except rolling fields and open sky. As it was, she'd be making a trek back to the inn, and would have to scramble to get dinner finished in time. Missing laelaps or not, she'd still would have a crowd to feed.

"I think this is probably where we part," Bev said with a mournful sigh. "Have to get back."

"I'm so sorry we didn't find Biscuit," PJ said with a frown. "I wish we could stay and help."

"No, no. You've done plenty. Thank you for searching with me. It's better that you two get on the road," Bev said with a smile. "You weren't kidding about those soldiers. I wonder where they're staying?"

"To the south," Grant said. "I saw 'em when I left Dane's this morning. Whole big group of 'em."

"Oh, goodness. Maybe Her Majesty's finally arrived," Bev said. It would certainly be a little relief from the anticipation, though what she brought might be worse. "Doubly good for you two to go."

"I'll be sure to write this time," PJ said. "And do let me know if you find...*when* you find Biscuit."

"I will." Bev forced a smile. "And you two keep to your studies, all right? It's important you learn as much as you can."

Grant snorted. "You sound like Bardoff."

"Well, he's got a good idea every once in a while," Bev said with a chuckle. "Take care of yourself. And maybe stay off the roads until Her Majesty's forces get a little less…"

Hoofbeats on the ground drew all their attention, and Bev swallowed as a pair of soldiers came riding up on horseback. But as soon as they were close enough, she relaxed. "Oh, hello again! Ollie and Casimir, wasn't it?"

They'd been in town with Zed Mackey during the solstice and were somewhat friendly. She'd also saved one of their own from being permanently changed into a tree, and their commander from a gingerbread fate, so Bev felt a little less nervous around them. The two boys didn't feel the same, tensing and shifting nervously.

"Hello again, Bev." Ollie hopped off his horse. "What are you three doing out this way?"

"Was walking these two young men out of town," Bev said, hoping Grant and PJ would leave this to her. "This is PJ Norris and Grant Hamblin." She snapped her fingers. "Grant's sister Vicky was briefly engaged to Allen, Zed's son."

They nodded, eyeing the two teens suspiciously. "And why are they leaving town?"

"Back to school," Bev said. "They're studying at the university there in Sheepsburg. Came back a few days for the festival, but they've got some tests coming up they need to prepare for. Right, boys?"

"Yes, sir," PJ said, his voice still ringed with tension.

"Do you have any proof of these studies?" Casimir asked.

Bev furrowed her brow. "Why do you need proof? Isn't my word good enough?"

"Unfortunately, no. We've got orders from Duke Bombadom not to let anyone leave without cause." He at least looked pained to say it. "So—"

"I've got our enrollment papers here," PJ said, reaching into his bag and pulling them out. He gave Bev a meaningful look, like perhaps he'd expected something like this, then handed them over.

"Odd that you'd have these traveling," Ollie said.

"I actually forgot them at home before we left," he said, sounding like he was thinking quickly. "Luckily, I was able to still enroll, but they do need these."

"Your parents didn't think to mail them to you?"

"Goodness, Ollie, you asked for proof, and they gave it to you," Bev said, giving the soldier a sideways look. "Now, I've told you they've got to get on their way. It's a long way to Sheepsburg and as it is, they'll probably be still traveling when night falls. I don't think I have to tell you what two young men might encounter on the road when the sun goes down. Why don't we let them go, hm?" She paused. "I would be happy to provide even more proof to Zed or Duke Bombadom if needed."

There was a long pause, and the two soldiers conferred silently, then Ollie nodded. "Fine, sorry, Bev. They can go."

"Right, boys." Bev hugged them tightly. "So you'll write to me?"

"As soon as we get there," PJ said with a tight smile.

"Be safe. And hurry up."

The boys gave the soldiers one final look before hoisting their bags and setting off down the road. Bev stood there for a moment, waiting until they were over the first hill, before turning back to the soldiers.

"Well, it is good to see the two of you," Bev said, hoping to change the subject. "Are you lot in town with Her Majesty?"

"She's not here yet, but we understand it will be soon," Casimir said. "Come, we'll walk you back to town."

"That's not necessary," Bev said, waving them off.

"We insist."

Chapter Thirteen

It was less an offer and more an order, and Bev said little as they escorted her back into town. She kept looking for any sign of Biscuit but kept her searching discreet. The soldiers would probably hear about Biscuit's attack eventually, but she didn't want to hasten their discovery.

"Has Karolina told you we have a few folks who've gone missing?" Bev asked, looking up at them. "Dane Sterling, a farmer, and Rustin?"

"No, she hasn't."

"Well, she doesn't seem keen on doing anything about it," Bev said. "But maybe the two of you could look into it—"

"We have our orders."

"Yes, I'm sure you do. But Karolina fired Rustin because he wasn't doing his job, and now *she's* not doing *her* job, so one would think—"

"Rustin was fired for not properly dealing with a magical element in town," Casimir said, keeping his eyes on the road.

Bev waited for him to elaborate, but he remained silent. They certainly seemed much more tense and tight-lipped than they'd been at the solstice. She could've charitably attributed it to the queen's arrival, but as they continued on in silence, she found she wasn't feeling all that charitable.

"Well, thank you so much for the escort back," Bev said, as they approached the inn. The livestock judging had clearly ended, because the town was once more flush with festivalgoers. "Do tell Zed to pop by the inn when he gets a chance. It'll be nice to see him again."

"I wouldn't leave town again, Bev," Ollie said, his tone clipped. "Someone might think you're up to something."

"What's that supposed to mean?" Bev said, putting her hands on her hips. "I told you, I was walking the boys out—"

They didn't answer, turning their horses and going the other way without saying goodbye.

"Bev?" Allen stepped out of the bakery, concern on his face. "What's going on? Who are *those* soldiers?"

"They work for Zed, actually," Bev said lightly. "Has he been by to see you?"

Allen shook his head. "I barely even saw him during the solstice when he was in town. He seems to want to go back to pretending I don't exist, which suits me just fine." He nudged her. "Why were they escorting you back?"

"We crossed paths while I was walking Grant and PJ to the edge of town. They're going back to Sheepsburg."

"Already?" Allen furrowed his brow. "Vicky said they weren't planning to leave for ages, and she told me they were leaving together."

Bev rocked on her heels. "I think they found the presence of the soldiers a bit unnerving. Wanted to get back to their studies."

"Grant probably just didn't want to be in the wrong place at the wrong time," Allen said. "He's not changed one bit, you know. Still selfish."

"I think he's matured," Bev said. "He's sticking to PJ like glue."

"PJ's not any better, though. Both of 'em."

Bev started, remembering Allen didn't know about PJ's magical abilities. "Right. Well, they're on their way back in any case. Glad I was with them, because those soldiers stopped us, asking where they were going. I was able to smooth things over so the boys could continue, but they insisted on escorting me back to town."

"Why were you even walking them?" Allen asked.

"I was looking for Biscuit," Bev said, briefly explaining what had happened.

Allen's face darkened. "I bet you a whole gold coin that Bombadom was sniffing around where he shouldn't have been, and *that's* why he got bit. Biscuit's not one to fly off the handle like that. The only time I've seen him growl is at a queen's soldier."

"You're probably right, but Bombadom's too high-ranking for me to do anything about it," Bev said.

"What do you mean? He's a Harvest Festival judge, isn't he?"

Bev told him what she'd learned from Andres, and his scowl grew even deeper. "That explains what happened this morning. I went to drop off Etheldra's baked goods, like I do every morning, and the shop was closed. When I asked Vicky, she said Shasta was told by Bombadom they weren't allowed to open until he'd finished his *inquiry*."

"Inquiry?" Bev frowned, remembering Etheldra had argued with Bombadom the night before. "What kind of inquiry?"

"I don't know, but I'm sure it has nothing to do with all the iron tea the twins have been drinking," Allen said. "Poor Shasta's about at her wit's end at the apothecary. She's tested nearly every day. Hope

Bombadom leaves *her* alone, or she's likely to snap."

Bev glanced at the bakery. "Has he been by yours yet?"

"Not yet." Allen sighed. "I keep hoping being Zed's son might afford me some protection against him, but that might just be wishful thinking."

"You should consider drinking some iron-infused tea yourself," Bev said. "Where's Lillie?"

"Doing deliveries," Allen said. "She wanted to get out of town for a bit. The increase in soldiers was making her nervous."

"Hope she can get back *into* town," Bev muttered. "It seems the soldiers are patrolling the farmlands and roads, and turning back anyone who might be leaving. But maybe with a wagon full of pastries, Lillie could prove she had business elsewhere."

"Well, what about all the people coming and going from the Harvest Festival?" Allen said, throwing his hand in the air. "Are they checking all those folks, too?"

Bev could only imagine the headaches. "I hope not. Maybe PJ, Grant, and I were just unlucky—or maybe they've got orders to keep an eye on me."

"Bad luck for you, but good for the festival," Allen said with a half-smile. "I can't imagine asking everyone who they are and where they're going has any benefit to the queen."

"Unless they're trying to ensure the magical folk

can't escape," Bev said. "When Lillie gets back, tell her she's got a place at Merv's. Might be safest for her to stay there for a bit."

Allen nodded. "I'll keep an eye out for Biscuit, too. I'm sure he hasn't gone very far." He squeezed her shoulder. "Chin up, Bev. We've only got a few days left of this madness. Then things will go back to normal."

~

Bev had very little faith things *would* go back to normal, but she went about making dinner anyway. It was strange to move about the kitchen without a little ball of fur underfoot, and she found she had way more potato skins to take to the compost pile than usual. In vain, she inspected her pile to look for any signs Biscuit had been by to eat, but it was just as high as it had been.

"Oh, Biscuit, where did you go?"

Even with her mind elsewhere, she assembled dinner, and at six, Bev brought the first of several platters out to a crowd half the size she'd been expecting. But they seemed hungry, so she ducked back into the kitchen to get the side dishes of mashed potatoes and the vegetables that had cooked with the meat, along with some extra roasted parsnips, not to mention the two kinds of bread. She smiled at the queue, before realizing Etheldra and Earl weren't first in line. In fact, there were more than a few soldiers in the mix, most of whom said nothing but crowded at the same table.

Finally, a familiar face joined the queue. Bev smiled at Max, hoping he might know why they hadn't shown up for dinner.

"I don't know," Max said. "I haven't seen them all day. But I haven't been out and about, either." He glanced at the table filled with soldiers. "Best for me to keep a low profile, if you get my meaning."

"I do," Bev said. "Allen said the tea shop was closed, and there was some kind of investigation. I just hope nothing's gone too wrong."

"I hadn't heard that," Max said, looking concerned. "I know she and that judge got into it last night, but—"

"She needs to watch her tongue," Bardoff said, coming up behind Max. "Being so rude to Duke Bombadom. We need to give deference to all members of Her Majesty's services, but today I found out that we've got a *duke* in our midst. And one of Queen Meandra's favorites, too." He puffed his chest as if he were a bird. "I wish I'd known who he was sooner. I could've welcomed him with the children's song and performances. He wouldn't mind seeing it twice when Her Majesty arrives, I'm sure."

"He should be here for dinner at some point," Bev said, her smile thin. She, personally, wasn't looking forward to seeing him. "So, you really haven't seen Etheldra or Earl all day, Max?"

"No. Are you worried about them?"

Bev hesitated. She wasn't one to jump to conclusions, but with Dane, Rustin, and Shamus missing, she felt compelled to make sure the couple hadn't joined them.

"I'm just going to check on them," Bev said, looking around the room. Everyone had already been served and was tucking in. "Would you two mind keeping an eye on things for me?"

"Nothing'll happen while these soldiers are here," Bardoff said with a sideways look.

"But we'll make sure nothing goes awry," Max said, nudging Bardoff.

With that sorted, Bev disappeared through the back door. She hurried through the town until she came to Etheldra's small cottage. There was a light shining in the window, but Bev wouldn't be happy until she saw their faces.

She rapped on the door. "Earl? Etheldra? Are you there? It's Bev."

The knob turned over, and Earl appeared, much to Bev's relief. "Bev? What's going on? Is everything all right?"

Bev put her hand to her chest. "Goodness, I was worried about you. It's not like you to not show up for dinner, and—"

"You can thank that *perfidious* judge for that," Etheldra snarled, coming to stand next to Earl. "Do you know what he did today?"

"I heard your shop was closed," Bev said with a nod. "For how long?"

"Until the inquiry is finished." She snorted. "But I know it's all a sham. First, that Bumblebrain came in saying I didn't have the right licenses, and demanded gold. So I told 'im to bring me an official note from *Her Majesty* that said he was authorized to demand it. Next thing I know, he's sniffing around my garden, telling me my plants seem *off* and that he's sent them off for testing."

"Oh, Etheldra." Bev put her hand to her chest. "Do you think—"

"My plants are as regular as the weeds in front of the house," Etheldra said. "It's my skill with *combining* them that makes my tea what it is, you know. But that's a hard thing to test for."

"Still, she's not allowed to operate until he's satisfied," Earl finished with a sad shake of his head.

"And I think that'll be a long time, yet. Doesn't like being told *no*, that Bumblebrain."

"Bombadom," Bev corrected mildly. "He can't keep you shut down forever, though."

"Watch him." She shook her head. "But I'd decided I'd had enough of this nonsense. Got kicked out of the pie-making contest, too, by his friend, so there's no reason to stick around. Told Shasta to mind the shop until I got back, and we'd set out to the south, but..." She pursed her lips. "We were turned back by *Zed Mackey's* soldiers."

"I encountered them myself," Bev said with a sigh.

"They told me I'm not allowed to leave until my *inquiry* is closed." She eyed Bev. "And why are you here, anyway? And without bringing me any rosemary bread, either."

Bev perhaps should've grabbed them a slice or two; she had plenty. "Well, with Rustin and Dane Sterling going missing, I just wanted to make sure something similar hadn't befallen the two of you."

"No progress on that front, eh?" Etheldra said.

"None," Bev said. "And worse yet—Biscuit's gone missing." She told them about him attacking Bombadom, earning a righteous cheer from Etheldra.

"I knew that dog was smarter than the average mutt," she said with a gleam in her eye. "I'm sure he's just fine, Bev. Probably found a new compost pile to keep himself fat and happy on until things blow over."

"Yes, but I don't think I'll be able to rest until he's on *my* compost pile," Bev said. "Since you're staying in town, would you mind keeping an eye out for him?"

"Of course," Earl said. "And thank you for coming by to check on us, Bev. Glad to know we've still got some good friends in town."

~

Bev's return to the inn was much slower, as she

was both relieved the couple were fine and concerned that they'd been turned back. Bombadom's actions had been wholly unfair, but Bev wasn't sure who she could bring a grievance to. He was, unfortunately, the most high-ranking person in town, and considering Bev's dog had 'attacked him earlier in the day, Bev probably shouldn't be poking the bear any more than she already had, so to speak.

She didn't walk through the front door, instead opting to peer in the window. The crowd had thinned out considerably, except for the soldiers, who were still eating. But Bombadom and Warford had finally arrived and were serving themselves. Max had already left, but Bardoff was seated in Bev's usual spot, talking animatedly to the two judges. Although their backs were to Bev, she could almost picture their reactions, and it gave her a small bit of pleasure to think of them being forced to listen to Bardoff's off-key singing.

She circled to the back and walked in the kitchen door, taking a moment to search her root cellar, compost bin, and stable once more for her missing laelaps before pumping water to start the dishes.

While she worked, Bardoff's chipper voice echoed from the front room, along with dwindling conversation from the diners. She didn't want to chance a look out the front until she was sure

Bombadom had left. When his deep voice announced his departure to bed, she exhaled—then gave it five more minutes before she walked out.

"Ah, Bev! Everything all right at Earl and Etheldra's?" Bardoff asked.

"Yes, yes. They're fine." Bev beamed at him. "Thank you so much for keeping an eye on things for me."

"It was my pleasure, I assure you. I was able to get a nice long chat in with our incredible judges and greet Duke Bombadom properly. He was so kind, telling me he couldn't possibly take the honor of being the first to hear the children's performance away from the queen."

"Oh, he did, did he?" Bev said, struggling to keep a straight face. "What a lamb."

"He did mention," Bardoff said, glancing to the floor, "that he'd had an unpleasant encounter with your dog."

Bev cringed. "Is he still sore about that?"

"I'm afraid so," he said. "He was happy the dog wasn't around anymore, but he did say he was going to bring it to Ms. Hunter's attention in the morning."

"He hasn't already?" Bev would've thought that would've been his first stop.

"No, apparently, he was already quite busy ensuring the town meets all Her Majesty's expectations," Bardoff said, gazing up at the staircase as if it were the queen herself. "What a boon it is to have him in town. I can't imagine how embarrassed I'd be if Queen Meandra arrived and started pointing out all the inconsistencies and problems."

"I don't see how Etheldra's shop is a problem, Bardoff," Bev said, some of her neutral facade falling. "Apparently, she asked him why she needed to have licenses and pay gold, and next thing she knew, she's being accused of having magic."

"Well, Duke Bombadom is just trying to make sure everything's all right. If she doesn't have magic, there's nothing to worry about."

"Except her shop is shut down in the last busy week before the winter months." Not that Etheldra had complained about that, but it still was a good point. "It seems retaliatory."

"Agree to disagree," Bardoff said, grabbing his cloak and wrapping it around himself. "Ms. Etheldra has always had too sharp an opinion for my liking, so maybe this is a good lesson that some of those opinions are better kept to herself."

Chapter Fourteen

Bev didn't think one brush with Duke Bombadom would be enough to change Etheldra after sixty-odd years, but she let that go. She was just grateful she'd avoided speaking with him, and was able to get the inn back in order in peace. Of course, she slept fitfully, as there wasn't a warm ball of fur nestled between her legs, and when she awoke, she felt his missing presence acutely, especially when she went out to feed Sin.

"I'm sure he'll come back," Bev muttered, giving her some oats. "He's got to come back. Maybe Bombadom will have forgotten about it by this morning."

But when the judges came down first thing,

Bombadom's hand was still wrapped in a bandage, and his scowl at seeing Bev deepened considerably. She wondered if a laelaps bite was a different sort of injury than a regular dog's but stopped herself from hoping so.

"Good morning," Bev said. "Did you sleep well?"

"As well as can be expected with this awful wound on my hand," Bombadom said. "Is that mongrel still about?"

"He seems to have run off," Bev said, keeping her tone neutral. "I haven't been able to locate him since putting him out yesterday afternoon."

"Hmph." Bombadom looked around, as if expecting Biscuit to jump out at any moment. "Good."

"I still think it's important to alert the authorities about such a dangerous animal," Warford said.

"And I shall, indeed," Bombadom said. "Good *day*, Ms. Bev."

The two strolled out the door, and Bev exhaled loudly. At least they'd left before the morning pastries arrived, which meant Bev could chat with Lillie about going to Merv's without them overhearing. The pobyd arrived a few minutes later, carrying a basket and looking wide-eyed and nervous.

"Morning," Bev said. "How are you?"

"Wishing I'd just continued on yesterday," Lillie said, putting the basket on the counter. "I saw the judges leaving. Is there anyone else here who—"

"I think we're safe," Bev said. "What happened yesterday?"

"I delivered all the cakes and pies, no problem. But on my way back, I was interrogated by a pair of soldiers who wanted to know everything about me. Goodness, I thought they might pull out a magical tester right then and there." She cleared her throat. "Then when I got back, Allen told me what you'd said about Merv. I packed my things and went to go there but…"

"Let me guess, you were turned back?" Bev suggested.

She nodded. "Of course, I didn't have a good excuse to be out there, so I came back. But now… Bev, now I wish I'd just gone to Silverkeep. This place feels like it's closing in, you know? I daresay I saw more soldiers than festivalgoers yesterday."

"Probably because they're turning them away," Bev said. "I hope the pumpkin farmers can get through today. Though at least Herman and Trent will be able to enter their gourds."

"Goodness, those judges are going to have a field day with Herman," Lillie muttered. "That pumpkin isn't normal."

The front door opened, and Ida stormed in, looking like she hadn't slept in days. She walked right up to the counter and snatched one of the muffins out of the basket, stuffing it in her mouth before sighing.

"Good morning to you, too," Bev said. "Everything all right, Ida?"

"Two days. Today and tomorrow. Then it's over." She inhaled and exhaled. "It's been one thing after another, this year. I've half a mind to believe Bombadom was sent by Miranda Twinsly to ruin everything, but I don't think she's that cruel."

"Agreed," Bev said.

"Have another muffin," Lillie said, offering it to Ida.

The butcher took a bite, and the tension in her shoulders relaxed. Bev glared at Lillie, who sheepishly grinned.

"Oh, yes, that one hit the spot," Ida said with a sigh. "Thank you, Lillie. I don't know what you put in your confections, but they're always incredible." She swallowed. "Just don't tell Allen I said that."

"My lips are sealed," Lillie said. "Well, since I'm not going anywhere, might as well…get back to work." She sighed. "Yes. Just back to work. Until something happens, and I can't work…might as well work."

Ida watched Lillie curiously as she walked out the door. "What's going on with her?"

"She unfortunately ran afoul of some of the soldiers patrolling the border of town," Bev said.

"Have you had any interaction with them? Are they letting the festivalgoers come in?"

Ida nodded. "If they have a ticket. That's what I was doing all day yesterday—handing out tickets to everyone in town who was staying in Middleburg. It's quite the ordeal, but at least it's something. I think the vendors might revolt if the crowd got any smaller." She put her hand over her forehead. "Hendry wants me to stand at the main road from Middleburg and ensure that people can get in. Which means I can't help oversee the pumpkin judging." She gave Bev a sideways look. "Do you think you could cover that for me?"

"I would, but I'm trying to avoid spending any time in the same space as Bombadom," Bev said, telling her what had happened with Biscuit. "He still hasn't gone to see Karolina, and I'm hoping as long as Biscuit stays…well, missing, he won't."

"Bev, I'm so sorry," Ida said. "I'm sure he's just gone somewhere to hide out, you know? He'll be back." She tilted her head. "But I really need someone to help out with the pumpkin contest."

Bev sighed. "Fine. I'll handle it."

~

When Bev arrived at the town hall a few hours later, neither Warford nor Bombadom were there. But orange gourds lined the center aisle, guarded fiercely by their farmers. The pumpkins all came up to her mid-thigh—except the one at the front, which was almost taller than Bev. Herman, the proud owner, stood in front of it like he expected one of the other farmers to destroy it if he blinked too much.

It was, to be sure, a valid concern, as Claude's pig had smashed his entry last year. And just a month before, Bev had initially thought he and Trent had been poisoned because they were entering the pumpkin contest. She smiled at each of the farmers they'd hauled in for questioning, and none looked pleased to be there—least of all Trent.

"He cheated," Trent muttered as Bev walked by. "Gonna tell that judge, too."

"Don't cause trouble, please," Bev said. "Herman did nothing except grow his pumpkin on his land, same as you."

"Yeah, but there was a lot of magic under his land. Not fair."

Bev turned to him fully. "Trent, we have enough problems right now, and we don't need you adding to them. Now if Warford finds fault with Herman, that's his own business. But we don't need you starting anything, understand?"

He sniffed.

"I'm going to take that as a yes."

The judges arrived via a side door, with Warford leading the way, and Bombadom looking bored. Bev kept her gaze on the latter, wondering what he'd been up to today. There weren't that many more shops in town for him to close down, so maybe he was bored because he had no more gold to steal.

That was uncharitable, Bev thought to herself.

"Yes, well," Warford began, gazing around the room. "This is certainly a collection. I want to inform everyone that we will be testing each entry for any signs of magical tampering. I also want to know all about your growing process, and what kind of fertilizer was used." His gaze landed on Herman's pumpkin. "And please know that it's within my right to disqualify anyone who I deem to have cheated with illegal substances."

Herman puffed out his chest. "I didn't *cheat*."

"That remains to be seen." He finally noticed Bev in the corner. "What are you doing here? Where is Ms. Witzel?"

"She's having to help with the crowd control coming into town," Bev said. "I'm on the festival committee, too, so she asked me to sit in."

"But you're in the bread contest," Warford said, raising his brow. "This is highly unusual."

"I'm here as a representative," Bev said. "I don't think—"

"No, per the regulations, you can have *nothing* to do with the judging," Warford said, red creeping up his neck. "Obviously, you should have—"

"We did read it." Hendry appeared from her office. "Ida must've forgotten that Bev was in the bread contest. I'm happy to serve as the representative." She crossed the room to sit next to Bev. "Please, continue."

Warford, who looked like he'd rather cancel the entire thing, sniffed and turned to the first farmer. Their conversation was too quiet for Bev to hear, so she leaned over to Hendry and asked, "Why didn't Ida volunteer you first?"

"I don't think our poor Ida is thinking clearly. These judges have been *difficult* to please, to say the least." She tsked. "I won't admit this to anyone but you, but this festival's been a nightmare. Worse than Twinsly's meddling last year, even."

That was certainly a statement. "What do you make of Bombadom?"

"I make that he's here to help Warford," she said, evenly.

Bev quirked a brow. "And?"

"And I know my place, so I'm not going to say any more than that." She nodded to the front. "Here we go."

Warford had reached Herman, and the farmer puffed out his chest. Every head turned toward the duo, and even Bev's breath caught in her throat as she waited for the fireworks to inevitably begin.

Herman, too, seemed anxious, shifting his weight back and forth as Warford examined his overly large entry.

"This is…certainly a pumpkin," Warford began. "Do tell me what sort of fertilizer you used."

Herman, who'd presumably heard Warford ask the same question of the others before him, was ready with an answer. "I can't tell you *exactly,* as there are folks here who'd steal it and use it for their own pumpkins next year. But, erm, mostly it's from my compost pile."

"And what, exactly, do you put in your compost pile?" Warford asked.

"Vegetable scraps?" He seemed confused by the question. "I didn't cheat, if that's what you're asking. Nor did I use anything illegal. I just planted my seeds in the spring like everyone else, watered and fed the plants, and here we are."

"Yes, but there is a *marked* difference between their pumpkins and yours," Warford said. He pulled out a small device that looked like a corkscrew. Then he jammed it into the pumpkin, earning a gasp of horror from Herman.

"What's the big idea?" he bellowed.

"The pumpkin contest is happening now," Warford said. "There's no need to get upset. I'm merely testing your gourd for traces of...*magic.*"

Bombadom, who'd been silent before, narrowed his gaze.

Warford removed the corkscrew and brought the pumpkin flesh over to the front table, where Mayor Hendry usually sat during town meetings. He placed the sample on the table then pulled a vial from his pocket, tilting it so a single drop landed on the pumpkin.

Hendry winced when it sizzled.

"W-what does that mean?" Herman said, color creeping up his neck. "I ain't done nothing wrong. I don't know—"

"I'm terribly sorry, Mr. Monday, but it appears there are illegal substances in your pumpkin," Warford said, not looking sorry at all. "Mayor Hendry, please fetch Karolina Hunter."

The color now drained from Herman's face, and he swayed on his feet. "W-why do you need to get her?"

"Why do you think?" Warford said. "Now please, move out of the way. And don't cause a fuss, either. We must be respectful of our fellow contestants."

"He's innocent," Trent said, stepping forward. "And for me to say that is saying something, because he's a no-good cur, but he doesn't have a lick of magic in him. Never has, never will."

"The test results say differently. And if you'd like, we can test *your* pumpkin to see what comes of it, if you're so keen on defending your friend." Warford turned again to Hendry, who hadn't moved. "Mayor Hendry? Did you not hear me?"

Bev turned to Hendry, who was considering her options. Then she stood woodenly and walked out without a word, her boots echoing in the silent space.

"Now, where were we?" Warford said, wearing a smile as if he hadn't just called for Herman's arrest. "Yes, this one looks more normal…"

Bev was glued to her seat, though she kept a wary eye on the door. She didn't want to believe Hendry would get Karolina, but she *could* also see it. Hendry's first priority had always been protecting herself, as she would definitely be taken away if anyone found out about her empathetic powers. But Herman…he was innocent. Truly innocent.

Warford had just finished judging the last of the pumpkins when Karolina walked in with Hendry trailing her, gaze cast downward.

"Ah, good." Warford nodded to Herman, who was sitting with his head in his hands with Trent and August Greenfield beside him. "Do take him away. His pumpkin very clearly has excess amounts of magic, through some kind of spell, potion, or cheating, so—"

"I swear, I didn't!" Herman cried, coming to his feet. "I don't really know why they got so big. But everything on that side of town was getting big, you know? The solstice made everything grow bigger."

"That seems unlikely," Warford said with a snort.

Hendry caught Bev's gaze and nodded toward Karolina.

Bev caught her meaning, hope flooding her

chest. "It's true," she said, coming to her feet to stand next to Herman. "Ms. Hunter knows all about the magical river in Pigsend, don't you?"

Karolina's nostrils flared. "Yes," she ground out.

"Herman's farm is right next to Alice's," Bev said. "And Alice's farm is where you…erm…" She cleared her throat. "Well, you know."

Another nostril flare, this time in silence.

"Not only that, but the solstice this year coincided with a full moon," Bev said. "And Herman's right, we had an overabundance of produce. You can ask anyone in town—Zed Mackey, even." More hope filled her. Zed could absolutely corroborate her story. "His soldiers even questioned Herman at the time and found nothing amiss. You can't fault a man for simply living on a magical river."

"I can, actually," Warford said. "As it's clear he used the river to gain unfair advantage over everyone else. Besides that, magic is *illegal*. All of it. No exceptions."

"Yes, except if we *stopped* the river, the town of Pigsend would fall into a sinkhole," Bev continued, gesturing to Karolina. "So what do you expect us to do?"

Bombadom was silent. Bev chanced a look at Karolina, who was breathing hard as she balled her fists. Bev had truly gone out on a limb to remind the soldier of the damage she'd caused in town, and it could backfire on her. But it would be awfully hypocritical of her to arrest Herman.

"Then the town should fall into an abyss," Warford said, earning a gasp of horror from those gathered. "There is no excuse for magic. Right, Mr. Bombadom?"

Karolina's gaze swept to the quiet judge in the corner, and to Bev's horror, he nodded. The soldier snorted and marched over to Herman, grabbing him by the arm.

"W-wait!" he cried, grabbing Trent's arm. "I'm innocent! I didn't do anything wrong!"

But Karolina was stronger, yanking him away and all but dragging him out of the town hall. Trent watched him, panting and red-eyed, before collapsing to the bench in tears.

"Fear not, Mr. Scrawl," Warford said. "It appears you've won."

Chapter Fifteen

Trent ignored Warford, turning to march out the door. The other farmers followed. Bev shared a look with Hendry then headed in that direction, too. But not before Warford tutted and commented on the idiocy of local farmers.

Bev walked out of the town hall and found Trent standing at the bottom of the steps, unsure what to do. She approached slowly then gently patted him on the shoulder.

"I'm sure he's just going for…questioning," Bev said. "Karolina knows what I said was true. Herman didn't do a thing wrong. I'm sure we'll find him back at his house before sundown."

Trent just nodded and shuffled forward.

Bev put her hands on her hips, tutting. Karolina wasn't going to take Herman all the way to… wherever those accused of magic went. She had a hunch the officer would take Herman to Zed Mackey's people, and *they'd* escort Herman. If she could get hold of Zed, maybe he'd be more reasonable than Warford or Bombadom.

She asked several vendors, and finally got confirmation the group had gone south. Odd, considering that was where the queen was supposed to be making camp. Whenever she arrived, of course.

Bev had no choice but to follow, keeping a healthy distance and walking out of town behind them. A pang of sadness hit her chest as she remembered her trusty laelaps was missing—and wouldn't be able to come to her rescue should something go awry.

"Just have to keep my own head on straight, I suppose," Bev whispered to herself.

They'd left Pigsend, and the close-in farms, and were now walking along a dirt road lined with trees and bushes. Bev veered off the road, still able to make a good pace through the trees, and more than once had to duck behind a bush when Karolina turned her head. But it seemed the soldier didn't see her, as she turned and kept almost-dragging Herman.

Bev couldn't hear their conversation but based

on the rigid way Herman walked and the rapid movement of his mouth, he was presumably trying to convince Karolina of his innocence, and based on the way she didn't stop walking, it wasn't working.

The duo kept walking until they reached the clearing where Her Majesty was supposed to be staying. Bev had thought it empty, but it was actually filled with tents. There wasn't one fit for a queen—they were mostly the same small white sheet over a stick—but the number of soldiers gave Bev pause.

Especially when Ollie and two other soldiers came walking up to meet Karolina and Herman, who was still fighting against her grip.

Bev maneuvered closer through the trees and bushes, though there was still plenty of space between her vantage and the meeting. Herman had continued to plead his case, until Karolina barked at him to *be quiet* (which was so loud Bev heard it quite clearly).

The handoff happened then Karolina turned and walked back into town. Two of the soldiers marched Herman back toward camp, with Ollie following.

"Ollie!" Bev called, jogging over. "Wait up!"

All three soldiers stopped and turned, surprise evident on their faces. Herman, too, turned to her in shock. Bev's heart broke for him—it was clear he'd been crying.

"You can't arrest him," Bev said, a little

breathless as she approached. "He's innocent. He's done nothing wrong."

"Take him," Ollie said to the other two. "I'll deal with her."

Herman's face crumpled, but he allowed himself to be taken by the other soldier.

Ollie turned to Bev with an impatient sigh. "What do you want, Bev?"

"I want you to let that innocent man go," she said. "Warford said he'd cheated, used magic, but there was nothing except the magic under his farmland to enhance his pumpkin. It's cruel and unfair to blame him for what happens naturally."

He sighed. "The order came from Bombadom. We can't ignore a direct order from someone like him."

"What about Zed? Surely, he can—"

"Bombadom outranks Zed, too," he said. "Look, I don't really like it any more than you do. And most likely, we're gonna test him for magic, go to his house, test around there, and find that it's exactly as you describe. Then, once Bombadom leaves town, we'll probably let him go."

Bev exhaled. "Oh, thank goodness."

"Unless, of course, Bombadom says otherwise," Ollie said. "In which case, our hands are tied."

"I'll just have to convince him of Herman's innocence, then," Bev said, glaring at the campsite. A task made harder with Biscuit's attack, but she'd persist nonetheless.

Ollie turned to leave but gave her an appraising look. "You'd do well to stay on his good side. You're already well known enough in Queen's Capital. One wrong step, and you might be in Herman's spot."

She bristled at the threat, but the sincerity in his eyes was clear. "I never try to get on anyone's bad side. But I can't help it if they do bad things." She paused, eyeing the tents. "Who else have you taken?"

"What?"

"Have you any other folks in those tents?" Bev asked. "Like Dane Sterling? Or Sheriff Rustin?"

"I haven't seen Rustin," he said with a shake of his head. "We also don't have anyone under arrest other than Herman."

Bev pursed her lips, scrutinizing him.

"I'm not lying to you, Bev," he said, holding up his hands. "I promise."

"Did you tell Zed that Rustin's missing?"

"Not yet," he said. "We've been busy—"

"Making sure no one comes and goes out of Pigsend and arresting innocent farmers who happen to live on a magical river," Bev said with a glare. "Such important work."

He had the good grace to look ashamed.

"Well, *do* tell Zed he needs to come by and see me, because if no one's going to stand up for the people of this town, I'm going to have to do it myself, even if it means I have to take my grievances directly to the queen whenever she arrives." Bev put her hands on her hips. "If she's ever *going* to arrive."

"I don't know any more than you do on that front," he said. "But I do promise to tell Zed you're asking for him."

Bev couldn't help but feel defeated as she returned to Pigsend. Ollie had given her small comfort that perhaps Herman would be all right, as there really was nothing to arrest him on. But Bombadom having the final say left her nervous and unmoored. How awful it was that one man decided the fate of everyone in Pigsend. But that was, perhaps, the same in Queen's Capital. Bev was grateful she'd never had the misfortune of visiting.

She still hadn't a clue if they'd found Shamus, or, worse, Biscuit, and she had *no* intention of sneaking around in their camp this evening. Trent's farm, the town hall, even a bar in Lower Pigsend were fine to break into and poke around. But she wasn't poking the bee's nest of an entire camp of soldiers. If Shamus *was* there, then he'd have to save himself. He was a wizard, after all. He could extract himself better than Bev could.

Her kitchen was inviting, if not empty without Biscuit there to greet her. Bev sank onto her stool, putting her head in her hands before glancing at the clock. Her bread was on the verge of being overproofed, so she quickly shaped the loaves and put them in their tins then went to get her meat order. She had little conversation for Hans, who'd heard through the grapevine about the happenings at the pumpkin contest.

"Outrageous what they're doing. Now you understand why we hate the queen's people, and everything she stands for."

Bev just nodded without a word, taking her order and bringing it across the street.

She worked through dinner, glancing at the spot in the corner more times than she wanted to admit. Biscuit had now been gone a whole day. None of the soldiers mentioned they were looking for Biscuit, nor had Karolina come asking for him, nor had anyone mentioned they'd caught him. Still, she would've much rather known he'd found somewhere safe to hide, unlike Herman, who was probably still sitting in the makeshift jail at the soldiers' camp.

Once again, she found herself facing the problem of one man being the be-all, end-all of justice—and the feeling Bombadom wasn't interested in *true* justice himself. But surely, with some more explanation—and perhaps a belly full of food—he'd understand that arresting someone for just living on top of a magical river was absolutely ridiculous.

But Bev wasn't the only one to have that idea.

When she brought out dinner, the entire roster of pumpkin-contest entrants sat at one of her tables, grim looks on their faces. Trent, who wore the biggest scowl of all, stood watching the front door, as if ready to attack Bombadom the moment he came inside.

"Dinner is served," she said, though it wasn't really necessary. Those who'd come to eat were already in line, and it was clear the pumpkin farmers had other business. None of them even looked at the spread of roasted pork, mashed potatoes, and roasted carrots, not to mention the rosemary bread.

"How's it going, Bev?" Reginald said.

"It's going," she said. "Glad to see you're still around. Business been good for you this festival?"

"Bah. If I sell half of what I brought, I'll be doing well," he said. "Everyone's on edge this week. No one's opening their purses, as they're worried they may be stopped and robbed blind by one of them soldiers."

"The soldiers aren't robbing people," Bev said with a smile. Then, thinking about it, she asked, "Are they?"

"Figure of speech," he said. "Only one who seems to want to rob people is—"

The two judges strolled in just at that moment, catching the attention of everyone there. The pumpkin farmers rose, but deferred to Trent, who was screwing up his courage. Puffing out his chest, he strode toward Bombadom and blocked his path.

"Can I help you?" Bombadom asked.

"I want to talk to you about Herman," he said. "He's innocent."

"I find it quite difficult to believe you would vouch for him," Warford said. "If he was innocent, he would be taking home first place."

"Yeah? That don't matter to me." He put his hands on his hips. "Herman didn't cheat. He got lucky, I guess, living on that magical river or whatever Bev said, but he didn't do no more than the rest of us."

Warford's upper lip curled. "Then we'll be sure to test the rest of you, too. Her Majesty has no tolerance for any kind of magic. Herman's pumpkin was found with it, and therefore, he must suffer the consequences." He turned to Bombadom. "Right?"

Bombadom nodded. "He will be adjudicated as anyone else in this country would after being found with magic. The terms of his incarceration and release will be decided by a judge in Queen's Capital. This is the law of the land, and we must follow it."

Trent growled, taking a threatening step forward. "And what if we don't want to follow the law of the land, eh? We were doing just fine before your crowd showed up and made a mess of things. Taking gold from hard-working folk, shutting down our farmers' market and our flour mill. You lot won't be satisfied until everyone in Pigsend is bled dry, will you?"

"Trent." August, one of the other farmers, came up beside him, putting his hand on his arm. "I think it's time we get you home."

"Yes, that's wise," Warford said. "There's quite a significant punishment for threatening a member of the queen's service, you know. I'd hate to send another pumpkin farmer down to Commander Mackey's camp to the south."

Trent stood his ground. "Then send me. Herman don't deserve to be arrested, but if you're gonna do it, might as well arrest me for something real."

"Trent," Bev said, walking to the door. "Time to go."

It took two farmers to drag him out, but they managed it. Bev didn't doubt he'd willingly go down to Zed's to plead Herman's case or keep his sometime-friend-sometime-nemesis company. But she also figured he'd get the same reaction she had.

"It's no use," Bev told him once the door to the inn closed. "They're following orders. But he's going to come out innocent, I know it. And when he does, they'll let him go."

Trent didn't seem convinced, but he made no move to walk back inside. "They're a bunch of crooks, you know. All of 'em. I never joined the army—too old—but after the way they've treated us, I might just sign up. Better than getting stepped on."

With that, he stormed off, thankfully toward his own house, though there was a good chance he'd turn south toward Zed's. If he did, Bev just hoped he kept his temper.

She came back inside, finding the room quiet. Warford sat alone at the table the pumpkin farmers had vacated, eating his food. The rest of the diners had piled their half-eaten plates on the table and made their way out the door behind Bev. She hated to waste so much food, but she understood why they didn't want to stay.

"Did Mr. Bombadom retire?" Bev asked.

Warford took his time answering, slowly slicing his meat. Bev noted that once again he hadn't grabbed a slice of rosemary bread. When he finished chewing and swallowing, he finally answered, "I believe he went for a stroll."

Bev turned. She'd been standing at the front door for the past few minutes. "Out the back?"

"Are there more doors in this inn?" He snorted as he took his knife to his meat again. "I do plan on writing to my superiors about the treatment we've gotten in this place. I was told there was a great deal of anti-regal sentiment out here, but I can't believe how much I've encountered."

That might have something to do with the amount of gold you're collecting. "If you'll excuse me, I'm going to start cleaning."

Bev took a stack of plates to the kitchen, but after depositing them in the sink, she rushed out the back door. She squinted into the darkness, wishing once again that she had her trusty laelaps to help her find Bombadom. But as she walked down the street a bit, she spotted a figure in the moonlight—so she followed him.

Chapter Sixteen

Bev had become something of a professional in the art of following someone. Bombadom didn't seem to have a destination in mind (at least, based on his leisurely pace), but Bev wanted to keep an eye on him anyway. He walked right past the thick patch of trees where Bev had found her missing amulet, not giving it a second glance. But when he turned westward, Bev had a hunch he might be going to speak with Zed.

The commander was waiting in the moonlight, and saluted stiffly when Bombadom approached. It took Bev a bit to find a good spot to eavesdrop—helped by a cloud sweeping over the moon—but eventually, she was able to crouch behind a bush close enough to catch their conversation.

"…I don't think arresting Herman Monday was necessary," Zed said, before adding, "Sir."

"You know as well as I do Her Majesty requires order in her realms," Bombadom said. "This farmer's pumpkin was chock-full of magic. I can't even believe he submitted it into the competition. Surely, if he had the year before, the previous judges should've picked up on it and barred him from competing."

Zed sighed. "Pigsend's had a magical river beneath it since before it was founded. You can't stop it or the ground becomes unstable."

"Then the people should be moved, and the river stopped. Magic is outlawed—even natural forms. It's too dangerous for any one person to wield. You, most of all, should know this and appreciate that I've isolated another potentially dangerous magic user." Bombadom sniffed. "Unless you're having second thoughts about your alliance with Her Majesty?"

Zed took a step back. "I've been nothing but loyal to her since the moment I defected. I believe in the cause. There's room for some nuance—"

"Magic is evil. End of story."

Bev waited for Zed to continue, but he remained silent. The wind blew, rustling the leaves around her and sending a chill down her spine. She wasn't sure what the two men were waiting on until

Bombadom spoke again.

"Here comes Ms. Hunter. Finally. You should be sure to remind her it's important to be prompt."

Bev turned in her hiding spot just in time to duck more. Karolina walked right by her, but thankfully, didn't notice the crouching innkeeper in the bushes. She looked her usual disgruntled self, even as she saluted her two superiors.

"Commander, Duke Bombadom. Apologies for my lateness." She didn't offer an excuse or reason. Perhaps she knew it wouldn't be accepted. "What can I do for the two of you?"

Bombadom looked annoyed to be ordered around thusly, but he spoke evenly. "Commander Mackey tells me during the solstice, an effort was made to test the townsfolk for magic."

"Yes, but we gave the job to Rustin," Zed said, showing no signs he knew the sheriff was missing. "So it wasn't done well."

In fact, he'd given the list of people to test to Bev, and instead of testing them, she'd brought them bits of a strawberry rhubarb crumble infused with iron and willow bark so they'd have some relief from the surging magic of the river beneath them—and so they'd pass any test Zed meted out.

"I was looking at our records before I arrived here. Besides that one failure at the solstice, there don't seem to have been any other attempts at comprehensive testing, just a piecemeal approach, with anyone who overtly *showed* signs of magic being tested. But I've seen more suspicious behavior than I'd care to admit over the past few days. It would be good to test every person, just to ensure we haven't missed anyone hiding in plain sight."

Bev winced. *That* wasn't good. Andres's warning about her making an iron-infused crumble came back, and she wished she'd taken it more seriously.

"I'm not sure that's entirely necessary," Zed said. "Last time I was in town, there was a plethora of magic that could've enhanced anyone's natural ability. I didn't see anyone worth mentioning, so I doubt there's anyone in Pigsend with anything interesting."

"Then perhaps you should've looked harder," Bombadom said. "That innkeeper, specifically, seems to be up to no good."

Bev scowled at him. She hadn't been anything but nice to the judge since he'd arrived—even taking his side when Biscuit attacked him.

"Bev?" Zed shook his head. "She's…well, I'm honestly not sure what to make of her. But she's an ally."

"I doubt that." Bombadom sniffed.

"Likewise," Karolina drawled. "She's nothing but a pain in the rear. Gets herself into situations she shouldn't be in. She disrupted my queen-sanctioned search of the town last year—"

Bev scowled. *Because your search was causing*

sinkholes. But she was more interested to see if Bombadom mentioned Biscuit—so far, he hadn't told anyone.

"She also saved my life at the solstice," Zed said. "I think she knows more than she lets on, but I don't think she's our enemy."

"Be that as it may," Bombadom said. "Ms. Hunter, I'm tasking you with the job of testing every villager in Pigsend—the locals and the visitors. Anyone who even elicits a spark on the test should be brought directly to Commander Mackey's encampment."

"We don't have room for that," Zed said. "We're here as a peacekeeping mission only, providing support to Her Majesty's forces."

Bombadom paused, and the air around the trio tensed. "Are you disobeying a direct order, Commander Mackey? Do you have sympathies for the magical folks in your old hometown?"

"N-No," he said, sounding nervous for the first time. "No. Of course not. I just need a few hours to reorganize."

"You have until sunup, as that's when I want Ms. Hunter to begin testing people," Bombadom said. "And believe me: if those tents are empty by the time testing is done, I will have something to say to Her Majesty about your loyalty, Mackey."

~

Bev waited until the trio was long gone before

even taking a breath. Bombadom truly was an awful person, and whatever his true intentions for Pigsend, he wanted every magical person out of the way. She placed her hand to her chest, worrying about Ida and Etheldra and the Brewer twins. Mayor Hendry. Even Allen, Zed's own son, wouldn't be safe. She halfway wished the young baker had lost his powers after the solstice like everyone else. Lillie certainly wouldn't pass the test; but with all the soldiers, could she sneak out of town to Merv's?

She bit her lip. Hans Silver, too, would be in trouble. Gore might be fine, as long as he continued working in the forge, but how specific was the test? Would it find a single drop of magic, the shadows left behind by the overflowing magical river? What about the others who'd only shown magic during the solstice?

The risk was too great to hope for the best.

When the coast was completely clear, Bev hopped to her feet, a mission in mind. She'd have to work all night, probably, but she'd make a crumble with her satchel of willow bark and iron. But just as soon as the thought came to her, she deflated. She didn't really have anything to put *in* the dessert. She'd stocked up on potatoes, carrots, and the like for her side dishes, but she didn't have any apples or anything like that. The berries of the summer were long gone, except in jams and preserves.

In the distance, the moon shone on the town hall clock tower.

"Pumpkin it is."

Bev wasn't surprised the town hall had been left open nor that all the entries remained where they'd been. Bombadom and Warford certainly weren't going to take it upon themselves to clean anything up. Bev bypassed the humungous gourd Herman had entered, instead grabbing Trent's, which—while still large—was at least cartable. Though she became less and less convinced of that as her arms ached from the effort of carrying it back to the inn.

The front room was empty, so she returned to the kitchen. After sharpening her largest knife, she stabbed the pumpkin, carving it into large pieces and adding them to her biggest stock pot. When she'd filled the pot, she added enough water from the pump in the backyard to cover it, and stoked the fires underneath.

She opened one of her rarely-used drawers to locate the satchel of willow bark and iron. The willow was brittle and smelled faintly of apples and cranberries. How many times could she reuse the same piece before it wasn't effective anymore? She said a small prayer and tossed it in with the pumpkin.

While that heated up, she tackled the dishes, going back and forth to get more water until she had enough. She kept a wary gaze on the stove and the door to the front room. Before long, the pot was boiling, but the scents coming from it weren't all that exciting.

"Hm." Bev turned, trying to remember what sort of spices Allen added to his pumpkin goods. She ventured to her spices, most of which were dried herbs from her garden, and nothing that would go particularly well with pumpkin. Unfortunately, she was running low on sugar, too. So she snuck across the street to borrow some from Allen.

The baker's lights were out, so Bev found the key under the mat and let herself in. She scoured the rack of spices, grabbing cinnamon, allspice, cloves, and nutmeg, along with a large canister of sugar. But as she poked about, she heard a noise.

"Hello?" she whispered.

"Bev?" came a quiet voice.

"Lillie?" Bev nearly dropped the spices. "What are you doing here?"

Lillie emerged from the darkness, a bag slung over her shoulder. "I thought I might make a break for Merv's. But I needed supplies first." She opened her bag to reveal two bags of flour and sugar. "I'm not sure how long this'll last me, but hopefully long enough."

"Take some jam, too," Bev said.

"What are you doing?" Lillie asked. "Spices?"

"Another iron-infused dessert," Bev said. "And it's a good thing you're leaving, because Karolina's about to test everyone in town for magic."

Lillie shivered. "What's their problem?" she asked, keeping her voice low. "Why are they suddenly trying to ruin Pigsend? The war was six years ago."

"I don't know," Bev said with a sigh. "I don't know why Bombadom is the way he is, or what his motivation is, other than, perhaps lining his own pockets. But even that seems..." She shook her head. "There's got to be another reason for it. And I'd follow him around, but that's a harder ask when I don't have a laelaps to keep his scent for me."

"No sign of Biscuit, either?" Lillie frowned. "Oh, Bev, you must be so worried."

"I'm hopeful he's fine," she said, swallowing the lump in her chest.

"What are you going to make?" Lillie asked.

"I cut up one of the Harvest Festival pumpkins," Bev said. "Have it boiling with my iron nails now. Thought I might try a sweet bread. Do you reckon that'll work?"

"It should," Lillie said with a nod.

"You don't happen to have a recipe, do you?" Bev said. "I was scrambling a bit."

"No, but you can adapt that lemon-blueberry bread recipe you have. Substitute the pumpkin for the milk, but the rest should be more or less the same." She nodded to the spices. "And add those spices, of course. It sounds heavenly, to be honest."

"Well, I wasn't sure I'd be able to get away with a crisp again," Bev said. "I think Zed's becoming wise to my ways."

"Do you want me to stick around and help you bake it?" Lillie asked. "I could bring some to Merv, too. I'm sure he'd appreciate it."

"No, you need to get out of town," Bev said. "And be safe, all right?"

Lillie hugged Bev. "I'll see you soon. Hopefully."

~

Lillie disappeared into the night, and Bev returned to the inn, her mind whirring with all manner of worries. She would just have to hope that no news was good news where Lillie was concerned. A thick patch of clouds had moved in, which would help conceal her. And Percival's charms would keep the town of Lower Pigsend safe, too.

Putting Lillie from her mind, Bev stirred the stock pot of pumpkin flesh, finding it a bit too hard for her liking. Her trusty satchel had floated to the top, so Bev stuffed that back down into the bottom. She was so busy with her pot that she almost didn't hear the door open.

She braced herself, expecting Bombadom, but instead smiled. "Zed! Good evening. I heard you were back in town."

"Ollie told me you had something to tell me," Zed said, skipping the pleasantries entirely as he surveyed her across the kitchen.

"Ah, right." Bev wiped her hands and told him about Rustin and Dane's disappearances. "Ms. Hunter wasn't interested in looking into it. I doubt she's even been by their houses."

"She's busy," he said, looking around the kitchen. "Isn't it a little late to be making food? Dinner was hours ago."

"Well, funny story," Bev said, thinking quickly. "Apparently, Mr. Warford isn't a fan of rosemary."

He blinked. "What does that have to do with anything?"

"He's judging the bread-making contest," Bev said. "And if I want to win first place… I've been experimenting with different recipes. I tried rolls, but they're a bit harder to get right. I thought I might try a pumpkin bread, since they're in season."

"Mm." He walked to the stock pot and peered inside. "Where'd you get the pumpkin? The farmers' market's been shut down."

"Since the pumpkin contest is over, I just snagged one of the gourds from the town hall," Bev said. "It really was quite the event earlier." She paused, sure that he knew she'd been down to visit. "Has Herman been cleared yet? Ollie said once you'd investigated him, you'd find him innocent and let him go."

"I can't speak to his innocence, but we did pass him along," Zed said. "He's to be adjudicated elsewhere."

"I see." Bev's heart fell. "That's a shame. Everyone's quite worried about him. He didn't do anything wrong, either—"

"Bev, I came because I'm grateful for your help during the solstice a few months ago, so I thought I'd give you a heads-up on what's coming. The town's about to be inspected more thoroughly than it's ever been. Every person in town is going to be tested for magic—including yourself."

"Mr. Bombadom seems quite intent on finding someone magical in town, doesn't he?" Bev said. "What's his story, anyway? I'm not familiar with him."

"He's a duke in the queen's court. Been there for years. One of her favorites because of how ruthless he can be. No drop of magic is too little for him to take action against." He sighed. "While I'm of the opinion *people* shouldn't use magic, I personally don't agree with his decision on Herman. But I've been overruled."

Bev nodded. "Thank you for telling me. Not sure what I can do with this information, but—"

"I'm sure you'll do what you usually do," Zed said, turning to leave. "Karolina will begin in the morning. You've got a few hours between then and now." He glanced at the stockpot. "Good luck on your breadmaking contest. Rosemary or not, I'm sure you'll win."

Chapter Seventeen

Almost an hour later, Bev pulled three loaves of perfectly baked pumpkin bread from the oven. She placed them on the counter, hoping she wouldn't have to use her "I'm testing recipes so I'll win" line with anyone else—Bombadom probably wouldn't believe her.

She waited for the loaves to cool and finished washing dishes. It was going to be a long night, and she was already making a list of people who had to get a slice of bread from her. She worried she might not be able to wake people up, or that she'd make too much ruckus and arouse the wrong people. But as soon as she put the last dish away, there was a soft knock at her door.

"Bev?" Allen walked in, looking half asleep. "Lillie popped by on her way out of town. She told me I needed..." He nodded to the bread. "A slice of that."

"That was nice of her," Bev said. "Take one."

He wasn't out the door before Etheldra came in, wearing her dressing gown with her white hair pinned up. "I'm here for the—"

"On the kitchen table."

The Brewer twins were next, having been awoken by Etheldra, followed by Ida, who'd been awoken by Allen. Ramone, who'd been awoken by Ida, came next, wearing an extravagant silk head wrap and a sweeping cloak. There was a half-hour lull before the door opened again, and Gore and Hans came in to get their slices.

"Do you need it?" Bev asked Gore. "Haven't you been in the forge?"

"Can't be too careful," he said, walking out the door.

Hendry arrived looking like she'd spent hours on her hair and outfit. "Karolina's testing people, hm?" She pulled a slice toward her. "This isn't a wonderful development."

"Bombadom's orders," Bev said, keeping her voice low.

"Who's been by?"

Bev told her, and she nodded, seeming to count them off in her head. When Bev finished, she sighed heavily. "I *suppose* I should tell Wilda—"

"I'm right here." Wilda walked in, also in her dressing gown. "My dear former roommate was kind enough to alert me."

"I was getting around to it," Hendry said with a sneer.

Wilda stuck her tongue out at her and disappeared through the door.

"I believe that's everyone who has magic in town," Hendry said. "Unless you can think of anyone else?"

Lillie was safely at Merv's (or should've been by now). PJ was in Sheepsburg. Everyone who'd possibly need a slice had one.

But just as she'd had that thought, there was another soft rap at the door. Reginald, one of the vendors, came in with his hat in his hands. "Someone said there was, erm, special pumpkin bread to be had?"

Bev nodded to the table. "Help yourself."

He took another hesitant step inside. "And it'll… We'll pass the test?"

Bev shared a look with Hendry. "I can't guarantee it, but it's worked in the past."

"That's good enough for us."

"Us?"

Reginald turned behind him and waved, and soon there was a long queue of people lining up to get a slice. Bev had thought she'd have plenty left over, but when the last person walked through, she had nothing left but a few crumbs.

"Thanks again!" Reginald said, closing the door behind him.

"Well, goodness, that was unexpected," Hendry said. "Who would've thought there were so many *interesting* folks in our vendor corps?"

"It's quite nice everyone came here for a change," Bev said, picking up one of the larger crumbs and eating it. It was fantastically delicious—the perfect taste of fall. "Instead of me traipsing around."

"The people of Pigsend look out for each other," Hendry said. "Especially these days, when there's so much to look out for." Hendry rose and sighed. "Chin up. Karolina will do her test, everyone *should* pass, and we'll all be one step closer to being rid of all this drama."

~

Bev didn't sleep well—and it wasn't just that Biscuit wasn't there to keep her warm. She worried her infusion wouldn't be enough, or the bread's effects would wear off before people got tested. She replayed the conversation she'd overheard, as well as the one she'd had with Zed. Through it all, she kept coming back to the same idea: Bombadom was up to something more than just taking money. Perhaps the clue was his desire to stop the magical river under the town. At least he'd said they should clear everyone out before they did so, but that seemed more an afterthought.

Zed had once said the Battle of Eriwall, a gruesome battle that had turned the tide of the war, had changed his mind about his loyalty to the kingside and the people who wielded magic. Had Bombadom had the same experience? Had he run afoul of someone who wasn't so nice and that had led him to his current mindset?

She doubted the taciturn duke would say a word to her about it. Nor did it matter too much. He outranked everyone in town, and no one was able to argue their point with him. And something told Bev that if he was so beloved in the queen's court, Her Majesty had a similar point of view.

The morning came, and Bev was actually relieved that the final day of the Harvest Festival had arrived. She gratefully rose and started on her bread dough for the evening—as well as her contest-entry batch of dinner rolls. She would've liked to have made them one more time before the final day of the contest, but she'd had plenty on her plate.

When that was started, she continued with the rest of her chores, finding solace in the familiar routine. It was the only thing that hadn't changed in the last week, and she was grateful for the sound of Sin's bray and even the smell of her stall.

"At least you're still with me, old girl," Bev said, patting the mule on the nose.

Sin shook her head, stomping her feet.

"I'm all out of apples, I'm afraid," Bev said. "Farmers' market being shut down and all. But maybe I can take a trip over to—"

She stopped, realizing there was one person she hadn't seen last night. Bathilda Wormwood didn't have magic herself, but she'd been known to deal in magical creatures that Her Majesty would certainly find illegal. Bev hadn't really spoken to the older woman since the solstice, and there was no telling what she might be up to now.

"I'll pop by," Bev said. "Maybe go check on Alice, too. I'm sure they're all beside themselves."

Allen came, dropped off the morning pastries (which were breakfast biscuits, presumably because he hadn't gotten much sleep), and left without a word. Bev pushed the biscuits basket from side to side, idly remembering they were how Biscuit had gotten his name. She couldn't believe how much she missed the little devil, and not just because he'd been able to sniff out magic. She kept looking for a mischievous nose skimming the edge of her table, or listening for the sound of claws on her wooden floors. She'd even gone to the rug a few times to clean it, only to find it void of golden fur.

Thankfully, her sad thoughts were interrupted by Mandisa, Gena, and Ira coming down for the day. They gratefully took a biscuit and asked Bev if she was feeling confident about her chances this afternoon in the final contest.

"We'll see," Bev said with a shrug. "Who knows with the judges this year?"

"You said it," Ira grunted. "Not sure I'm going to come back next year, to be honest. The festival has changed—and not for the better. That judge, whatever his name is, seems to have taken the rules to a new level. Imagine, asking me where I sourced my yarn. As if I didn't raise the sheep and spin it myself."

Bev nodded, understandingly. "I hope he won't be coming back next year, myself. He seems..." She sighed. "Well, I just hope things get back to normal. Our festival's been run the same way for years now, and it doesn't seem right that someone from far off should blow through town and change it."

Ira nodded. "Hear, hear."

Bev smiled but thought to soften her tone just a hair. "I do try to remain diplomatic when it comes to my guests, but I've been forced to change my entry for the bread-making contest at the last minute. Those rolls I made the other night—"

"They were delightful!"

"That's my new entry," Bev said with a sigh. "I hope it impresses the judges. Goodness knows I was sore about missing out on first place last year. I'm sure Staunton Bucko's going to give me a run for my money again."

"I'm sure it will," Ira said with a nod as the last

two doors opened. He stiffened like he was about to be arrested. "Must be on my way. Want to get a good seat for the judging."

"Have a good one," Bev said, wishing she could join him. Instead, she plastered on the best smile she could muster as Warford and Bombadom walked down the stairs.

"There was quite a ruckus last night," Bombadom said, leveling an icy glare at Bev. "I overheard conversations well into the early morning hours. What in the world was going on?"

Bev hoped he hadn't heard the content of those conversations. "Just the usual late night Harvest Festival activity," she said, hoping that made sense. "You know how it goes. People stay up late, and they want to come and chat."

"I scented something baking last night," he continued, leveling an icy glare at Bev. "Did *that* have anything to do with the ruckus?"

"Yes and no," Bev said, thinking quickly. "I was testing recipes when a few people came by. Word got out that I'd made something delicious, and more people came. I daresay I barely have a crumb left after the crowd thinned."

"An odd time to test recipes," Warford said. "In the middle of the night."

"Well, I suppose I can thank you for that," Bev said, trying to keep her tone as pleasant as possible. "You told me you don't care for rosemary, and that's the best part of my bread, so I'm having to figure out something new. Thought a nice pumpkin bread might do the trick."

"Sweet breads aren't considered bread in the eyes of the contest," Warford said. "I hope you've made other arrangements."

Bev inwardly winced; she'd forgotten about that. "Yes, of course. I've got dinner rolls as well, if you'll remember. Were those allowable?"

Warford eyed the basket. "Are these them?" He picked one up and banged it on the table, leaving crumbs everywhere. "Hard as a rock."

"Those are breakfast biscuits," Bev said. "Something of a local delicacy here in Pigsend. You split them in half like this." She opened one. "Then add a slice of cheese and sausage on them." She layered them and replaced the top. "I think Allen put a nice jam in there, too, if you wanted to sweeten it up."

Neither judge looked impressed. "I'll pass," Bombadom drawled.

"Likewise," Warford said. "You know, it's quite a shame there aren't *two* meals served at this inn. A small bit of pastry from the bakery next door does not a meal make."

Bev bit her tongue instead of repeating what she'd *just* said about the biscuits, meat, and cheese.

"If I were to offer *feedback*, that's what it would be," Warford said with a sneer.

"I'll be sure to take that into consideration," Bev said. "But it would be nice to know if those dinner rolls I'm making back there will be allowed in this afternoon's contest…?"

Warford sniffed. "I suppose."

~

It was the first bit of good news Bev had heard in days. As soon as the judges were out the door, Bev spun on her heel and headed back into her kitchen to check on the rolls then skirted out the door, heading for Bathilda's. Her rolls would need a few hours to proof before she shaped them around midday, and she wanted to make sure Bathilda wasn't hiding anything suspicious before Karolina got there.

She walked briskly, passing Ramone's house and mentally checking them off, then Herman's farm, searching in vain for him. She said a small prayer that wherever he'd been taken, he'd be treated fairly and allowed to come home quickly.

After Herman's farm, Bev turned off the main road to walk the length of Bathilda's property. She'd had everything there from phoenixes to tanddaes, a sheep-like creature with magical purple wool. Bev spotted the thicket where Bathilda had been hiding her illegal sheep earlier in the year, and made a quick pass to ensure it was empty.

She walked up to the front door and knocked. "Bathilda? It's Bev. Are you there?"

There was movement on the other side of the door before it swung open, revealing a short woman with a scowl on her face. "What d'ya want?"

"Checking on you," Bev said. "Do you know about all the soldiers in town?"

"Aye." She sniffed. "They know better than to come by here. I'm just a farmer."

"Well, Karolina Hunter's been charged with testing everyone," Bev said. "For magic. Just wanted to let you know."

"How kind of you to give her a heads-up."

Bev stiffened. Karolina's voice echoed from behind them. She turned to find the de facto sheriff standing with two unfamiliar soldiers behind her.

Bathilda shifted. "What's all this?"

"As Ms. Bev indicated," Karolina said, "we're in the process of testing every citizen of Pigsend, per the orders of Duke Bombadom. So if you'll be so kind as to step out of your home, we will do our test and be on our way."

Bathilda hesitated, and Bev's stomach dropped. If only she'd been a few minutes faster. "Why do you need to test me?"

"Because we've been ordered to," Karolina said. "If you don't comply willingly, we'll simply have to take what we need by force."

"What do you need?" Bathilda said.

"Just your finger." She held out her hand. "If you please."

Her tone was pleasant, but the look on her face was anything but. Bathilda shared a nervous look with Bev then stepped forward. Bev could practically hear the thumping of her heart, and her stomach twisted in knots as Bathilda put her wrinkled hand into Karolina's.

The soldier pricked her finger with the tester Bev had seen Zed use at the solstice. The drop of blood went to the pinhead and, to Bev's horror, sizzled.

"Hm." Karolina didn't let go of Bathilda's hand. "What a shame."

"N-now wait a minute," Bathilda said, taking a step back. "You don't... That test is defective. I don't have a drop of magic in my body!"

"Then clearly there's magic somewhere in your house," Karolina said, looking at the other soldiers. "Search it. Find whatever it is she's hiding."

Bathilda took a step back, yanking her hand out of Karolina's. The other woman smiled, as if she knew Bathilda wasn't going very far, but then Bathilda put her fingers to her lips.

A loud squawking echoed from inside the house. Then there was a loud *boom*, and Bev cowered as bits of wood showered down on her. She scrambled off the deck as the house looked like a giant fireball had blown through it.

But that fireball swooped down and grabbed Bathilda by the shoulders, lifting her up and flying into the sky.

"What is that?" Karolina yelped as she cowered.

Bev hid a smile. Bathilda didn't seem to have gotten rid of that confounded phoenix after all.

The firebird carried the old woman higher and higher into the sky before the two of them disappeared over the horizon.

Chapter Eighteen

"Since *when* does Pigsend have *phoenixes?*" Karolina demanded. Her hair was covered in wood splinters, and the two soldiers with her were similarly befuddled by the turn of events. "And how long have *you* known about it?"

"Me?" Bev laughed. "Why would you think I knew about that?"

"Because you know *everything* in town," Karolina said, marching up to Bev.

"I don't know *everything*," Bev said with a shake of her head.

"Then why'd you come here?" Karolina asked. "You clearly knew something, because you were coming to warn Bathilda about the testing."

Bev thought quickly. "Bathilda's been a bit ornery lately. I didn't want her to meet you with a crossbow, so I thought I'd warn her you were on your way." Bev gestured to the destroyed house, which was aflame and falling down. "Obviously, her new overprotectiveness made sense. I had no clue she had a phoenix."

That was true; Bev had thought Bathilda had sold it to Winston to be housed in Lower Pigsend.

Karolina narrowed her gaze. "How kind of you to think of me."

"Well, to be honest, she pointed it at me a few weeks ago," Bev said. "And it wasn't pleasant." She nodded to the farm on the other side of the fence. "In any case, I'm headed over to Alice's next to pick up some vegetables for dinner. The lovely Mr. Warford shut down our farmers' market, so I'm having to go to the farms directly to get my goods."

"Shopping for produce without your wagon?" Karolina asked.

"Sin wasn't feeling well today," Bev said. "She's getting up there in age."

Silence stretched out between them, and Bev was *sure* Karolina was going to press, but instead, the soldier just smiled. "Fine. Let's *all* go to Alice's."

"Wonderful," Bev replied, hoping Alice didn't have a secret magical ability she hadn't told anyone about. "You can help me carry the potatoes back."

The quartet walked in silence, with Bev doing

her best to project an air of calm. Karolina kept glancing toward the sky, perhaps looking for the phoenix that had disappeared with the old woman, or perhaps searching for any more surprises that might drop from the clouds overhead.

Bev marched right up to Alice's house and knocked. When there wasn't an answer, she beckoned the soldiers to follow her, as she assumed the old farmer might be in her fields. She was in her barn, the same one PJ had destroyed during his first throes of shifting, with Holly and Pip Norris, shoeing her horse.

"B-Bev," Alice said, standing up straight. "What's all this?"

Holly looked at Bev with fear in her eyes, and Bev mustered a smile. "Well, *I'm* here to ask if you've got any apples or produce you want to sell me. Ms. Hunter and her friends have their own agenda." She cleared her throat. "We met up at Bathilda's, and they asked to walk with me."

"I…see…" Pip said, looking between the three soldiers and Bev. She could practically read the relief on his face that his son was back in Sheepsburg. Bev couldn't even imagine what would've happened if he'd stayed in town. "Well, Ms. Hunter, what can we do for you?"

"I need to test all of you for magic," Karolina said, glaring at Bev.

"We don't have any of that," Alice said.

"Though I hear that didn't matter when you arrested Herman yesterday."

"I need your hands," Karolina said. "Please."

Alice stepped forward to be tested first, glaring at Karolina as she held out her calloused hand. Karolina pricked it, and to Bev's immense relief, nothing happened. She supposed only living on the magical river didn't really infuse that much magic into someone's veins (except during the solstice).

"You two," Karolina said. "And your son, where's he?"

"Back at school," Holly said, her voice unusually high. "He didn't find the festival that exciting this year. Can't imagine why…"

"Fine. I'll just test you, then." She walked up to Pip first. "Hand."

He held it out, his pulse throbbing in his ear. The dragon-shifter grannies had said that the shifter gene had skipped a few generations, as Pip and Holly didn't have any sort of magic. But was this test so sensitive that it would show up?

Thankfully, Pip was clear.

"Now you." Karolina looked at Holly. Everyone held their collective breaths again, but thankfully, Holly's blood was normal, too.

"There?" Bev said. "Happy? Now, Alice, why don't we see about that produce? I'm about to run out of food at the inn, and I daresay Etheldra will be upset if I don't have enough for her."

"Can't have that," Alice said with a too-high laugh. "Right this way. Erm—"

"We'll finish up here," Holly said, quickly. "We'll get the payment later."

Bev looked at Karolina, who hadn't moved. "Anything else you need from us, Ms. Hunter? If you're going to test everyone in town, you should probably get a move on, hm?"

She'd said it while looking at the soldier, but hoped Pip and Holly got the message and would share it with anyone else who might need to know. She wrapped her arm through Alice's, and all but led the farmer out of the barn and into the sunlight.

"Lovely day, isn't it?" Bev said. "Now, where can we find those vegetables?"

"Bev, what in the world is going on?" Alice whispered.

"Just need to get that produce," Bev said, giving her a wink.

She waited until they were far enough away from the barn, and until the soldiers had departed empty-handed, before finally telling Alice the truth.

Alice's face turned red as she shook her head angrily. "Those monsters. Think they run the world. Coming here and testing us. As if we hadn't already gone through this six years ago." She sniffed. "But I just heard a loud noise coming from Bathilda's. Is she all right?"

"Um..." Bev nodded. "Well, she's all right. Her

house isn't. Long story, though. Better not to ask questions." She smiled brightly at Alice's confused face. "She'll probably be back in the spring. I'm sure she's gone for a long overdue holiday."

"Too much nonsense happening in town," Alice said. "First, we get sent away from the Harvest Festival. Then, we're told we can't sell our own goods at our own market. Now, they're coming to test us for magic? Are they trying to run everyone out of town? Is that their goal?"

Bev honestly didn't have an answer for her. "All I know is that you and the Norrises are in the clear. So at least you three can sleep easy tonight."

~

Bev purchased a crate of carrots, apples, and potatoes from Alice, who was very happy to get the gold, and promised to be back in a few days to get some more. She brought the produce back to the inn, leaving the crate in the kitchen before venturing out again. She stopped by the bakery first, to check on Allen, and he told her Karolina had already been by.

"Came in with a couple of sour-faced goons," he said, showing her his finger, which he'd bandaged to work with the dough. "Didn't say a word. I didn't even try to tell her Zed was my father. Not sure it would've worked."

Bev had to agree with that, but she was grateful he'd passed. "Did you see where they went?"

He pointed toward the butcher shop, so Bev went there next. But it was closed. Ida, presumably, was off doing festival things, and Vellora was probably on a meat delivery. Bev headed into town, bypassing the square entirely, and heading to the tea shop.

There were a few people sitting at the tables, but the conversations were muted. Several of the people had bandages on their fingers as well.

"I take it Karolina's already been here," Bev asked, walking up to Shasta.

She nodded, holding up her own bandaged finger. "Everyone in here passed, thankfully." She winked at Bev. "Grateful for that bread last night."

"Glad it worked," Bev said. "Suppose they really are testing everyone."

"If you're currently in town, you'd better give up your finger," Shasta said. "And unfortunately, it seems no one's allowed to leave. Vicky tried to head back to Sheepsburg yesterday, and she was turned back."

"I forgot all about her," Bev said. "Do you think she—"

"We brought her back some bread," Shasta said. "She's always had an affinity for plants, like we have, but I don't know if it's just a preference or..." She lowered her voice. "Something else."

"Good call." Bev was glad the boys had left when they had. "Did you see where they went next?"

Not that Bev wanted to follow them, but if there was anyone else in their path who she might be able to warn (who wouldn't have a phoenix capable of growing ten sizes and flying them to safety), she would try.

Shasta thumbed toward the east. "That way, I guess. Probably to test Stella for the fifth time."

Bev headed toward Shasta's sister at the apothecary and found the girl with a similar bandage. "Can't imagine why they thought it necessary. Karolina's tested me to within an inch of my life every day since Bernard left." She sighed. "Ready for the lot to leave town."

Stella told Bev the trio had continued east, and Bev followed the trail out to the miller. Sonny was a dear friend, and Bev probably needed a bit of wheat to stock up for the winter. He, too, had a bandaged thumb, and seemed of the same mind about the group.

"It was bad enough when that perfidious Warford came in here, asking about my *licenses*," he snarled. "Tried to shut me down. Going to take all year to recoup what I lost. Grateful Mayor Hendry was able to front me some of it, but I'm not a man who lets his debts sit, you know?"

"They must've taken a lot, then," Bev said. "All for licenses?"

He sniffed. "And lining his own pockets, I'm

sure."

Bev asked if he saw where they'd gone, and he thumbed toward Trent and Dane's farms. Bev went to Trent's first, finding him in his fields with a bandaged hand and a scowl on his face.

"It's only because I gotta stick around and tend to Herman's farm that I didn't wallop 'em all," he said. "Coming here like I'm a criminal. They got a lot of nerve, you know."

"Where'd they go next?" Bev asked.

"Said they were headed to Dane's, even though I told 'em he wasn't around."

Bev also found that strange, but headed toward his farm anyway, if only to see what they were looking for. Maybe they just hadn't taken Trent's word for it, and assumed Dane was hiding out. But when Bev got there, she found the trio of soldiers standing on the front porch, dumping out the chest Bev and Grant had found in the attic.

"What's all this?" Bev asked.

"None of your concern," Karolina said, toeing the red and black fabric with a look of disgust. "Just clearing out some filth."

"Dane's not here," Bev said.

"Probably knew we were coming and ran off," Karolina said. "Had no idea there was such an evil creature living here in Pigsend."

"Evil?" Bev laughed. "Dane's not evil. He's a farmer. He—"

Karolina kicked the tunic on the ground. "Know what this is?"

"A now very dirty shirt."

"It's the colors of the King's Guard, an elite fighting force that destroyed more of Her Majesty's soldiers…" She sneered. "Amazing that he escaped justice."

That certainly explained why he'd left without warning. "I see. I had no idea. He'd grown up here, you know. This was his family farm—"

"I'm not interested in a history lesson," Karolina said. "I want to know where he went."

Bev plastered a neutral smile onto her face. "You and his cousin Grant. If you'll recall, I informed you that Mr. Sterling had gone missing a few days ago. You weren't, erm, *interested*."

Karolina's nostrils flared, and Bev sensed it might be time to head back to the inn.

"If you do locate him," she said, inching backward, "let me know so I can pen a note to Grant. I'm sure he'll also be surprised to learn his father's cousin's unique history. I daresay the kids found him quite dull."

"Why are you here anyway?" Karolina asked, eyeing her. "Hoping to give someone else a heads-up?"

"Yes. You. I wanted to let you know Mr. Sterling had been missing for several days, so coming to his farm would be fruitless." She gestured to the pile of clothes. "Clearly, I was mistaken, as you've found something quite interesting."

"Clearly."

"I've got to get back to the inn anyway," Bev said, thumbing the way she'd come. "Dinner doesn't make itself."

"We'll walk you."

~

Bev certainly didn't care for an escort, but she let the trio of soldiers walk her back to the inn, depositing her in her kitchen.

"You should probably avoid any more *jaunts*," Karolina said. "Someone might think you're up to something."

"Yes. Informing our illustrious sheriff that the farm she was inspecting was empty," Bev said with a serious nod. "I'll be sure to keep such important information to myself in the future."

Karolina narrowed her gaze. "If you leave this inn, I'll have to—"

"What? Arrest me?" Bev laughed. "On what charges?"

"I'll find something."

"Well, do forgive me," Bev said. "But I have to cross the street to check in with the butchers. You see, I make a meal for my guests every evening, which does include your superior Duke Bombadom. If I can't make it across the street—"

Karolina pinched the bridge of her nose and

gestured toward the door. "Fine. Go over there. But be back. Then you aren't to leave anymore."

"Fine, fine. I've got lots to tend to here anyway."

"And he's going with you." Karolina pointed to one of the two stone-faced goons.

"Well, come on, then," Bev said with a sigh.

The silent soldier followed her across the street, but when Bev tried to open the door, she found it locked. "That's...odd." She turned to the soldier, giving him a sideways look. "If you're charged with escorting me, then we've got to head into the festival to find Ida. I'm sure—"

"Bev!" Ida ran down the street. "Bev, goodness me, I'm so glad I found..." She slowed when she saw the soldier escort. "Erm, hello. What's all this?"

"Don't mind him," Bev said. "What's wrong? Something with the festival?"

Ida glanced at the soldier, chewing her lip. "It's not that, it's... Do you mind if we have a private word?"

"Yes." It was the only word the soldier had spoken since Bev had first met him.

Ida huffed. "Vellora wasn't in bed this morning. Didn't take the wagon, either. Hans didn't show up to open the shop. I just went down to his house to find him, and neither he nor Freddie is around. I'm not sure..." She shook her head. "Goodness, Bev. It's not like her to just disappear like that. I'm hoping it's not whatever took Dane and Rustin."

Ida's meaningful glance at the soldier was clear: *it* being the soldiers themselves. Bev had no clue how much of Vellora's secret work with Andres Ida knew about, but Ida had to have some kind of inkling, even if she didn't know the whole story.

"Well?" Bev turned to the soldier. "What do you think? Five people are missing now, if you count Dane and Rustin. Is that something you lot want to tackle, or am I going to be expected to?"

He glared at her then silently motioned for her to follow him. Before she could, Ida grabbed Bev's arm.

"Be *careful*, Bev. Something's not right," she whispered. "They won't hesitate to arrest you if they think they can get away with it."

"I'll be fine," Bev said. "But you might want to run over to Gore's and let him know."

Ida stared at her in confusion for a moment then nodded. "I-I'll do that. Thanks."

Chapter Nineteen

"So, no meat, then?" Karolina asked after Bev returned to the kitchen.

"Well, as one of my two butchers seems to be missing, and the other one is beside herself with worry, no," Bev said. "Suppose it's barley soup tonight. Etheldra's going to be furious."

"You don't seem very concerned about her well-being," Karolina said.

"I'm quite concerned," Bev said, checking on her bread dough under the tea towel. "But you don't seem to be. Or you'd be out walking the streets looking for her, as I was for Rustin and Dane when they first went missing."

Karolina rose leisurely. "Who all is missing

again?"

"Sheriff Rustin, Dane Sterling, now Vellora Witzel, and Freddie and Hans Silver," Bev said, counting them off on her hand. "With Dane and Rustin, I had nothing connecting them whatsoever. The only thing connecting Dane, Freddie, and Hans is they live near to each other, and Hans was helping Vellora with the butcher shop while Ida was busy with the festival. Rustin, I suppose you could say he was helping us with management of the festival, but that's quite a stretch."

Obviously, Bev didn't mention Biscuit's disappearance, nor Shamus's. But with the revelation about Dane's history, Bev was starting to see a very clear pattern. With the exception of Biscuit, everyone who'd gone missing was affiliated with Andres in one way or another. Had Andres lied to her about not knowing who Dane was? Clearly, they'd fought for the same side.

"She told the other woman to talk to a man named Gore," the soldier said.

Karolina quirked a brow at Bev. "Why?"

"Gore was Freddie's campaign manager during the last election. I'm not sure who else they're close with," Bev said, thinking quickly. "But I thought maybe Gore might know where they'd run off to."

"Goodness, you have been busy," Karolina said. "Well, it does seem like quite the ordeal, doesn't it? Unfortunately, we have our orders. And I have to suspect that all those folks who disappeared so suddenly might not have wanted to be tested."

"Oh, you know, you're probably right," Bev said, acting as if that were a reasonable idea. "I don't know if any of them would fail the test, though. Everyone around here's been pretty normal."

"Except that woman with the phoenix."

"Right, well." Bev chuckled. "As I said, Bathilda's been acting odd for the past few months, so I suppose we should've guessed she was up to something." Bev looked around the room. "Well? Is there anything else you'd like to know? Otherwise, I've got to start chopping vegetables for soup and finishing my bread for the contest this afternoon. Good thing I went to Alice's today to stock up."

Bev kept her face even but held her breath as she watched Karolina. The soldier seemed determined to pin something on Bev, but walked out of the inn, Ollie following.

Once they were gone, Bev exhaled and sank onto her stool, putting her head in her hands. She didn't doubt someone would be watching the inn to make sure she stuck around, so all she could do was peel vegetables anxiously and duck into her root cellar in the backyard to retrieve a bag of barley for the soup.

Just as she finished chopping the last carrot, Ida breezed in, looking harried and concerned. "Oh, thank goodness, you're alone. What is—"

"Don't ask," Bev said with a shake of her head. "Did you find Gore?"

"No," she said, chewing her thumb. "No, and Bev, I'm so worried. This isn't like Vel. And with those soldiers down south... You don't think they arrested her, do you?"

"Do they have cause to?"

"I don't know. It seems like they're just doing whatever they want without consequence," Ida said. "I thought with Zed back in town, there'd be some order, but it doesn't look that way. Warford's probably sent half of our fiber arts contestants home because they didn't have the right breed of sheep." She leaned on the table wearily. "Bev, this festival's been a disaster. I don't even know what to say about this afternoon's final food contest."

Bev wished she could offer comfort, deny the claim and say it had been wonderful, but she couldn't find it within herself to lie. "Next year will be better."

"Is there even going to *be* a Pigsend next year?" Ida asked. "Everyone's talking about these soldiers, and no one's seen the queen. The festival is *over* today. What if her arrival was just a ruse to get these soldiers here, and their goal was to clear out the town?"

"For what purpose, though?" Bev said.

"Maybe the queen wants to tap into the magic of the river," Ida said. "I've been thinking about it ever since Hendry told us she was coming. She likes to hoard all the magic for herself, doesn't she? Well, what if her goal is to make it so unbearable to live in Pigsend that everyone leaves—or is arrested—so she can suck up all the magic for herself, leaving the town in a great, big sinkhole?"

Bev started. "You know, Bombadom said something to that effect last night. That the town should be moved so the magical river can be drained."

Ida narrowed her gaze. "That's ridiculous. This town's been here for centuries. Farmland passed down from generation to generation. And they want us to just…what? Pack our belongings and move somewhere else so Pigsend can fall into a sinkhole?" She balled her fists. "I guess none of that matters to that woman. All she cares about is her own power and complete dominance over this land." She wiped away a tear. "Listen to me, sounding like my wife. She'd be so proud her rebellious tendencies finally rubbed off on me."

"Be sure to keep those to yourself for the foreseeable future." Bev put her finger to her lips then poked her head into the front room. Empty. Then she poked her head into the backyard. Also empty. Then she came back to Ida. "Tell me everything that happened last night. Anything at all that might explain where Vellora went."

"We'd barely spoken two words to each other all

week," Ida said. "I've been so busy with the festival. I just come home and fall asleep, and Vellora's up and gone before I'm awake. Last night, though… when Allen came to get me about the bread, Vellora popped upright and said she had to go."

"She went to Freddie and Hans's," Bev said, more to herself. "Then came home?"

"Yes, she came home after that," Ida said. "But why Freddie and… Do they have…?" She swallowed, shaking her head. "I don't want to know."

"Good idea," Bev said. "But she did come home after getting Freddie and Hans? Just want to make sure I've got the timing right."

"Yes," Ida said. "She was beside me when I fell asleep around midnight. But when I woke, she was gone. I thought she might've gone on meat deliveries, but our wagon was still there—and the meat was right where it had been. And her clothes… She didn't wear her usual clothes, either. I do all our laundry, and I know what she's got. Everything was there. So…" She swallowed.

"Has Vellora mentioned anything she's been doing with Andres lately?" Bev asked.

"No, but I had a feeling he was involved," Ida replied darkly. "She's been a bit quicker to criticize the queen's people, especially since that fiasco with Bernard. Vellora's never been so antsy in her life." She looked at Bev. "Where do you think she might've gone?"

"I don't know, but my hunch is that everyone's in the same spot," Bev said. "And we just have to hope it's nowhere near here."

~

There wasn't much Bev could do from the inn, but she told Ida to go on like normal, and they'd sort everything out as soon as it was feasible. Ida had to go monitor the jam and pie-making contests, not to mention the bread-making contest this afternoon. Bev busied herself with chopping vegetables and preparing for a meatless dinner. But if her vantage from the front room was to be believed, there probably wouldn't be that many diners coming. The only folks walking the streets wore Her Majesty's colors.

"What in the world is happening to Pigsend?" Bev muttered.

"We should remove everyone from the town." Bombadom had said it so flippantly, like he was describing cleaning mud off his shoes. Bev hadn't thought anything about it, but she was starting to wonder if Ida was right. It seemed so ludicrous, so insane to think that the queen would be so bold as to empty an entire town for her own selfish reasons, especially since Her Majesty was keen to end all magic.

Except that wasn't *exactly* true.

Bev put down one of the doughy rolls and

narrowed her gaze. A year ago, during the sinkholes, a group of gnomes had set up shop in the mountains, digging for magic for Her Majesty to use. At the time, they'd not found any, because Karolina had already put a stop to the magic for her own purposes. But what if there was a plan to remove all the citizens from Pigsend, have the gnomes come back and dig up all the magic for Her Majesty, then leave the town destroyed?

It seemed cruel, but Her Majesty had proven herself so.

With the rolls cut and shaped, and the rest of dinner ready for the oven, Bev opened the front door to the inn. She wasn't surprised to find her stone-faced, nameless soldier standing there, silently watching her and waiting for her to leave.

"I've got to enter my bread in the final contest in a few hours," Bev said, by way of warning him. "I do hope Ms. Hunter won't mind."

He didn't respond.

"Well, if you're lucky, you'll get a nice slice of bread from all the contestants," Bev said.

The minutes passed slowly, but soon enough, Bev was putting the rolls and rosemary bread into the oven. She paced the kitchen, watching the clock intensely as she counted down the time until she could pull out her rolls. It seemed such a silly thing to get worked up about, but it was something within her control, which had been in short supply of late.

Forty minutes passed, and Bev pulled the rolls from the oven, pleased with their color and size. She let them cool before slicing them into individual pieces and placing them in her basket. The rosemary bread was also finished, and she put those on the counter for dinner.

"Well, at least one thing went right today," she said to herself.

Confidently, she strolled to the front door again, where her stoic guard was still waiting. Bev said nothing to him and left the inn, unsurprised when he followed close behind. Together, they walked the nearly empty streets to the town square, which was…mostly empty.

Bev frowned. It seemed most of the vendors had already packed up and left—a day early.

"Well? Are you going to the contest?" came the voice of the soldier behind her.

"Y-yes, just wasn't expecting… Anyway." Bev adjusted the basket on her arm and kept walking. "Has Her Majesty arrived?"

"I'm sorry?"

"Well, it's the last contest on the last day of the festival," Bev said, eyeing him suspiciously. "It's her last chance."

He didn't respond.

"Hmph. So much for all the effort."

Bev marched into the town hall and found it

completely empty. A moment of panic passed across her chest, worried that she'd misremembered the time, but Ida popped out of Mayor Hendry's office, pale and harried.

"Hi, Bev. Um. I'm so sorry to tell you this—"

"It's been canceled?" Bev said.

"Apparently, all the other contestants were… from out of Pigsend, and weren't allowed to come in." She gave the soldier behind Bev a nervous look. "It's been happening all day. Unfortunately, Warford doesn't seem to… If they don't show up…"

"If more than fifty percent of the final entrants to a contest do not show up, the contest is forfeit," Warford said, popping up from one of the benches. "And seeing as it's four o'clock now, and only one of the five finalists has arrived, then that's that." He clapped his hands. "This concludes this year's Pigsend Harvest Festival."

"Well, isn't that wonderful?" Bev said, looking down at the basket and picking up a dinner roll, offering it to Ida. "Hungry?"

~

Bev and Ida walked back to their side of town together, with the soldier trailing behind. Ida, who wasn't very hungry, declined to take a roll, and so did the soldier, so Bev would just serve them for dinner. She was oddly unbothered by the current turn of events, perhaps because, on some level, she'd been expecting it.

"It doesn't look like these soldiers are going home any time soon," Ida muttered, as a quartet walked by them. "Oh, Bev, what's happening?"

"I don't know," she said.

"I'm so worried about Vellora. But I don't think I'm allowed to go look for her, am I?" Ida whispered, looking back at the soldier. "What if she's really in trouble?"

"She's a very capable woman," Bev said. "And she would never do anything to hurt you. Quite the opposite, in fact. I'm sure, wherever she is, she's itching to get back to you."

"I hope so," Ida said as they reached the butcher shop and inn. "Be careful over there."

"I'm just a simple innkeeper," Bev said with a shrug. "What could they have against me?"

The answer came when Bev walked into the inn and found Karolina and four soldiers waiting for her.

"Give me a few minutes to get dinner ready," she said. "Feel free to have these rolls. Apparently, the bread-making contest was canceled. My loss is your gain, I suppose."

But no one moved.

"What's wrong?" Bev said. "You are here to eat, aren't you?"

"You know, Zed told me *explicitly* that I wasn't allowed to test you," Karolina began with a malicious smile. "He said you probably wouldn't pass, but you had saved his life, and he owed you. So I didn't." She smiled. "That being said, you were told not to leave the inn. You violated a direct command from a member of the queen's service."

Bev crossed her arms over her chest. "I hardly think me going to the town hall to enter my dinner rolls into the Harvest Festival is worth all this."

"You were told explicitly. You ignored it. Ergo, as you're now under suspicion, I can test you without running afoul of Zed's orders." She smiled as if she'd been waiting for this for ages. "Hold out your hand."

Everything in Bev told her to ignore the order, to turn and leave. But there was some part of her that wanted to know. Needed to know. So she held out her hand.

The pin pricked her, and a drop of blood came out. It landed on the pinhead and sizzled and popped, as Bathilda's had.

"Well, well, well, look at that," Karolina said quietly. "Suspicions confirmed."

"And what suspicions are those?" Bev asked. "Because if you have something to share about my past, I'm all ears. I'd love to know where I come from."

Instead of answering, Karolina pulled a pair of iron cuffs from her back pocket. "Bev, or whatever your name is, you're under arrest for illegal possession of magic."

Chapter Twenty

Despite being under arrest, Bev was actually quite calm about the whole thing. She wasn't surprised about having magic—well, maybe a little —but still didn't know what that meant. She hoped someone might have an answer for her soon, because it was bothersome that everyone seemed to know the truth but her. That sense of curiosity overrode whatever other nervousness threatened to drown her, and she was able to keep a cool head. After all, there wasn't really much she could do about it. Best not to let her mind run wild with theories until she knew more.

Karolina was almost gleeful, parading her down the street. Ida came out of the butcher shop, her hands over her mouth. Allen, too, put down his pastry bag and ran outside, his mouth hanging open. Bev winked at both of them, if only to calm their fears, because she wasn't sure what else to do.

"Mind the inn for me, will you, Allen?" she called. "I'm sure we'll clear all this up shortly."

"I wouldn't be so sure about that," Karolina said.

They walked through the town square, where Hendry looked on with a stoic expression, and Bardoff, who was saying goodbye to the children for the day, jumped back in surprise. Max came running out of the library, but one look from Bev silenced him. She didn't want anyone getting in trouble on her account.

"Bev, no!" Earl cried, rushing out of his workshop. Etheldra was right behind him, her eyes missing their usual spark in favor of fear.

"It'll be fine," Bev said.

Vicky, Stella, and Shasta came running out of their home, Vicky's hands over her mouth. Apolinary came next, shaking her head. Holly and Pip, who were at Apolinary's house, gasped in horror. Bev was doubly glad Grant and PJ had left when they had.

Past the empty blacksmith shop, and Bev had to wonder if Shamus might appear out of nowhere and save her, as he had Bernard. Percival, of course, was locked away in Lower Pigsend, where he should be.

And Lillie, hopefully, was baking away at Merv's, with the moleman enjoying the fruits of her labor. Perhaps soon, all these soldiers would leave, and things would go back to normal.

For Bev, it felt like the end of a long journey, one she'd started six years ago when she'd stumbled into town with a gash on her forehead. There'd been signs and hints that this would be the ending, but she'd pressed on with baking and tending to her inn, hoping she'd be able to keep avoiding it.

Still, she was—hopefully—about to learn the truth. And that counted for a whole lot.

They kept marching south, toward Zed's encampment, and Bev nodded to Casimir and Ollie as they joined the ranks. Neither looked happy, so perhaps they'd been alerted of this new development ahead of time.

Karolina never strayed from her purpose, walking Bev right up to a large tent in the middle with a high flag on it.

Bev stopped, surprised for the first time. "Is Her Majesty here?"

"Keep walking," Ollie said, pushing her forward.

Bev found herself a little excited at the prospect. Clearly, the queen had missed the entirety of the Harvest Festival, but she was in town, and that was something. Bev glanced at her shirt, which had a few smears of flour, and wished she'd had the foresight to change.

But when the tent flaps opened, the only people inside, sitting at a table, were Zed and Bombadom.

Bev frowned, a little disappointed.

"Come on up," Zed said, his voice low and emotionless. "Let's get this over with."

The soldiers deposited Bev in front of the table and lined the tent, standing as if they expected her to make a break for it. Bev certainly had no plans to do that, and she smiled at them before turning back to her two judges.

"What is your last name?" Bombadom said, holding his quill ready.

"I don't know," Bev said. "Everyone just calls me Bev. But you can call me Beverage Wench, if you want."

Someone snickered behind her, but Zed's murderous glance put a stop to it.

"You've been found to be in possession of magic," Bombadom said. "How do you plead?"

"Not sure," Bev said. "I'm not sure if Zed—"

"Commander Mackey," he said, with a low growl.

"So sorry, *Commander Mackey* filled you in on my past. I arrived in town with no memory of who I was and where I came from, so I took a job at the inn. I confess, I have no idea what kind of magic you've found or why, but I'm not wholly surprised either."

"Yes, we thought that might be the case,"

Bombadom said, looking at Zed, who stood.

"I've devised a memory potion," he said, walking forward. "You will take this."

"Sure." Bev held out her hands. "Happy to."

She grabbed the vial and downed it in one motion. A tingling spread over her body, starting in her temples. But as she stared at Zed and Bombadom, the only thing that came to mind was that her brain tickled.

"I'm not sure that worked," Bev said. "Do you have something else?"

Bombadom glared at Zed. "You said that would work."

"I said it *might*," Zed snarled back. "I don't know what you found on her, or what type of magic, but whatever it is, I've never seen her so much as cast a single cleaning spell. My guess is that this is a wild goose chase."

"My test was very conclusive," Karolina said.

"Or were you just hoping it was?" Zed shot back. "You've had a vendetta against Bev since she outed you for causing the sinkholes."

"We're getting off track," Bombadom said. "Do you have another potion that could coax the truth out of her?"

"I've given you my strongest potion," Zed replied.

"Very well." Bombadom rose. "Then it's clear that we've exhausted the limits of the skills of the personnel we have. The next course of action is to bring this *innkeeper* to Queen's Capital for further testing and evaluation."

Bev's brows shot up. "Oh, really? I've never been there. Will I finally meet the queen?"

"Load her up," Bombadom said. "We leave now."

~

An iron-barred carriage waited for Bev, and she readily stepped inside. Bombadom seemed to want to keep a close eye on her, because his horse was right behind, and two of Karolina's stone-faced soldiers were on either side of her—but surprisingly, no one else. Zed and Karolina watched her with emotionless expressions, and Bev felt the oddest desire to wave goodbye to them.

Instead, she settled for squinting toward the distance, looking for any glimpse of Pigsend, as she got the feeling it might be the last time she saw it for a long time. The carriage rolled forward, and Bev sat back, resigned to her fate. But not quite done with Bombadom.

"So I'm curious," Bev announced, once they'd been on the road a bit.

Bombadom didn't respond.

"Was your goal to drain the town's river of magic? Or was it just to stop all magic? I confess, it's hard to figure your angle. And if you do drain the town of magic—"

"Stop talking."

"You've already got me under arrest," Bev said with a kind smile. "I'm surrounded by iron, for all the good it'll do you with my lack of magic. The least you could do is humor me on your motives."

"Motives?"

"Yes, see, I'm something of the resident mystery solver in Pigsend," Bev said. "Sinkholes, who's disrupting the Harvest Festival, blackmailers, destroyed buildings, cursed weddings, that sort of thing. It really was quite the busy year. Someone told me that everything in town was connected to a larger purpose. So, before I'm whisked away to spend the rest of my days in prison, you could at least do me the kindness of telling me *why* all those things happened."

"No."

Bev snorted. "Well, I do suppose torture's probably on the menu. And it will bug me to leave this grand mystery unfinished. But if you do let me in on the secret of who I used to be before Pigsend, that might be some balm to my—"

"Quiet down."

Bev pursed her lips. "Fine, I—"

She finally looked beyond the soldiers, realizing they hadn't gone that far out of town. In fact, they'd taken a large loop from the encampment to the south around to the empty fields to the north, and toward…

She sat up. "Why are we going to the dark forest?"

"I said quiet."

But Bev's pulse sped up as the carriage stopped at the edge of the forest. Going to Queen's Capital seemed obvious, but the dark forest? That concerned her more than anything.

The soldiers came around and opened the wagon door, but Bev didn't move.

"Where are we going?" Bev asked.

"Let's go."

Knowing if she didn't, they'd be a lot ruder than she'd prefer, Bev complied and scooted out of the wagon. She kept a wary eye on the forest in front of her, wondering what sort of treatment she'd get from the sentient thicket.

The soldiers flanked her on all sides as they approached the forest, and Bev held her breath. But to her surprise, the branches moved away, clearing a path for them. Did the dark forest secretly harbor an allegiance to Her Majesty?

They crossed the border, and the light from the outside dimmed. Magic tingled on her skin, and she wondered if the soldiers felt it, too.

Bark!

Bev froze, fear seizing her.

"Not now, Biscuit!" she muttered, looking around for her laelaps. Her gaze went to Bombadom, who'd clearly heard the bark, but...

didn't look concerned in the least. In fact, he didn't even *look* like himself, because he was…smiling?

The heaviness fell from her wrists as the handcuffs came off. As soon as they left her wrists, a pair of white paws landed on her thighs, and Biscuit smiled up at her, his whole body shaking with his frantic wagging tail.

"Biscuit!" Bev exclaimed, falling to her knees and sweeping him into her arms. He licked her face, which she realized was wet with tears. Curious, she sought out Bombadom again. "What in the world is going on?"

"Come on," he said, his voice much gentler than it had ever been. "We've got lots to talk about."

"What about—" Bev glanced at his hand, which had healed completely. "Biscuit attacked you."

"A misunderstanding," Bombadom said. "We've cleared it up, haven't we?"

Biscuit gave Bev another slobbery lick on the face.

"He missed you, that's for sure," Bombadom said.

"So you're the one who took him?" Bev said, picking up the laelaps protectively.

"No, he listened well when you sent him away. We simply crossed paths and came to an agreement. He's been here in the dark forest ever since. I'm sure he was planning to return to you when things calmed down."

Bev relaxed, but only a little. "I thought you'd left," she said to Biscuit, crushing him to her. "Didn't find a new owner, did you?"

"There's no way he'd do that," Bombadom said with a shake of his head. "Come on, let's see everyone else."

Biscuit wriggled in her arms, and Bev let him down. He pranced ahead, white-tipped tail bouncing in the dim light. Bev had never been so happy to be covered in golden fur.

Bombadom led her to the clearing in the dark forest where so many events had taken place. But to her surprise, it was completely empty.

"Everyone else?" Bev said. "Where's everyone else?"

"Look harder," Bombadom said.

Bev gave the clearing another look. Again, she saw nothing. Then, there were faint differences in the air, like how water distorts a reflection. The distortion became a figure, which became—

"Vellora!" Bev exclaimed. "Your wife is—"

"Absolutely beside herself, I'm sure," Vellora said with a sad shake of her head. "I'll be in trouble for a while yet for giving her a scare. But this was important."

The same distorted image was next to Vellora now, and as she stared at the space, Shamus came into view.

"And you!" Bev said. "The least you could've

done was let Percival know where you'd gone."

"He'll find someone else to man the clipboard," Shamus said with a snort.

Next to Shamus, another ripple revealed Dane Sterling, wearing a curious-looking brooch on his tunic. "You, too! Leaving without telling Grant where you'd gone."

"I'll be sure to write," he said. "But once I saw the soldiers coming into town, it was more important I disappeared."

"But why did you—" Another ripple beside him, then Gore, Hans, and Freddie appeared. "Hans, you told me you had no clue why Dane would leave?"

"Dane's been hiding some secrets, it seems," Hans said, apprising Dane with a smile. "Big ones. I daresay even Andres didn't know who he was."

"Where is..." She jumped as the final ripple made itself known, and Andres appeared wearing a bright grin.

"B-but you said...?" Bev stammered, the questions coming too quickly for her brain to process them.

"I'm sure you're confused," Andres said with a nod to Bombadom. "But we're here to clear everything up."

"Yes, considering you told me Bombadom was Her Majesty's favorite duke," Bev said and took in the sight of everyone assembled—and their weapons. "You're planning on launching an attack against the queen, aren't you?"

"The queen was never coming," Andres said. "That was a well-orchestrated rumor."

Bev turned to him, flummoxed. "How did you pull *that* off?"

"It wasn't Andres's rumor," Bombadom said with a grimace. "Unfortunately, it's the first step in the well-worn path of Her Majesty's soldiers infiltrating a village and removing every person in it so she can mine it for magic."

The zing of satisfaction Bev felt at being right was muted by her confusion. "You were terrorizing the town and taking money from business owners. You had Herman arrested! Am I to just look past all that because you're friends with Andres?"

"Herman is back home, keeping a low profile until the Harvest Festival's concluded," Bombadom said. "He was thoroughly tested and deemed to be without a trace of magic."

"You turned Etheldra and Earl back," Bev said. "And again, all that money you took—"

"A necessary evil," Bombadom said. "What I can get back to the townsfolk, I will, but the licensure and payment requirements come from Her Majesty. I have to take what she demands to keep up appearances."

"Appearances?" Bev said.

"I've been a spy in the queen's court since the

war," Bombadom said. "It took a long time to work my way into her inner circle, but I've never been able to shake the suspicions that my true loyalties lie elsewhere—especially from Zed."

"Grateful His Majesty never told that perfidious turncoat about you," Andres said with a glare.

"Zed did speak most ardently on my behalf just now," Bev said. "And he didn't want me tested, if that counts for anything."

"He's got a sense of right and wrong, but unfortunately, he's still loyal to the queen," Bombadom said.

Andres snorted.

"With Zed and Karolina Hunter in town, I had to play the part fully so as to not arouse their suspicions," Bombadom finished. "Which unfortunately, included taking money and closing down shops in Pigsend."

"That's awfully dangerous," Bev glared at him. "Especially making Karolina test everyone for magic."

"Andres assured me there was an industrious innkeeper who knew all the secrets in town, and who would ensure every single citizen would pass with flying colors."

Bev turned to Andres. "That's a big assumption."

"You've never proven me wrong before," he said. "And I did tell you to make an iron-infused dessert, didn't I? As I understand it, you made pumpkin this time. Wished I'd had a slice of that. I do love pumpkin."

"It was amazing," Hans said with an emphatic nod. "I hope you'll make it again."

Bev turned back to Andres. "I'm still confused. Why are you gathering now? And why during the Pigsend Harvest Festival, of all things?"

"The gathering was prompted by Her Majesty's decision to close Pigsend," Bombadom said. "And the festival brings in hundreds of folks from all over, which meant it was perhaps our last chance to slip in unnoticed."

"Why meet here?" Bev said. "Pigsend isn't anywhere special."

"Because we were summoned," Andres said, nodding toward a gap between Hans and Freddie. "By him."

Bev turned to the gap, focusing her gaze intensely until there was the ripple, then the figure, then…

"Rustin?" Bev blinked. "What in the…"

But it wasn't Rustin, except it was. His eyes were sharp and focused, his broad shoulders were steady and confident. And when she watched his face, it shifted and shimmered like there was *another* spell on it, morphing until the face staring back at her wasn't Rustin at all, but a completely unfamiliar man.

"Bev, may I formally introduce His Majesty, King Ferilious," Andres said.

Chapter Twenty~One

Everyone in the group bowed their heads, but Bev just couldn't fathom it. She scrutinized not-Rustin, looking for any signs of the familiar sheriff but finding none. If not for Biscuit's wagging tail whacking against her shin, she might've thought she was dreaming.

"But...but wait..." Bev shook her head. "But you grew up in Pigsend? Hendry said—"

"Sheriff Rustin did," he said with a nod. "But unfortunately, he never did manage to graduate from Her Majesty's services school. Instead, he moved to Percelville, several hours north of here, and is working as a dish cleaner under the name Kell Burns." King Ferilious smiled. "He asked no questions when he was approached by Dane, who he knew from his childhood. All he cared about was the tidy sum of money he received to change his life."

"And you've been pretending to be him all this time?" Bev asked. "Even going so far as to…pretend to be…erm…" How could she put this diplomatically? "A bit flighty?"

Ferilious laughed. "That was all real, I'm afraid."

"The safest place for the king to hide was right under Meandra's nose," Bombadom said. "The potion His Majesty took included the essence of the real Sheriff Rustin. Coupled with a befuddlement component, no one thought twice about bumbling, air-headed Sheriff Rustin—not even Zed Mackey." He smiled. "A credit, of course, to Andres's incredible skill."

Bev turned to Andres. "You told me—" She stopped. "Bombadom is the one who gave you the orders?"

Andres nodded. "I made the potion, but I was never told where the king was hidden, nor did I have any clue that your Sheriff Rustin was really His Majesty. Only Bombadom knew, and he alone was the one who carried the antidote to break the spell."

"Myself and, of course, Dane," Bombadom said, nodding to the farmer. "Picking Rustin as the double was his idea."

Bev looked between Dane and Andres. "You said

you didn't know who Dane was, Andres?"

"When Dane served under the king, he used a different name, perhaps to protect the family farm back in Pigsend," Andres said. "A boon, because he was able to resume an anonymous life and keep an eye on the king."

"And you two didn't know who he was, either?" Bev asked Hans and Freddie.

"Neither of us was old enough to fight in the war," Freddie said.

"And even if they had been, Dane's role wasn't well known by many people," Bombadom said. "He rarely left His Majesty's side. He was, perhaps, the best and only person to keep watch over His Majesty in his vulnerable state."

"Until it was time to wake him up, right?" Bev said.

Bombadom nodded. "I came to town the night before the festival and woke him. The potion was a bit of a shock, which explains the scene in his house."

"What did he dig up?" Bev asked.

Ferilious opened his palm, and a moment later, a glowing orb appeared. Magic crackled on Bev's skin, and she had to look away from it.

"This is what Karolina Hunter, Claude Renault, Dag Flanigan, and Zed Mackey have been searching for," he said. "It's the source of my power."

"So it wasn't my amulet," Bev said, with a

glance at Shamus. "The wizard's helper?"

"Her Majesty's soldiers wouldn't have even known it was there unless you held both pieces in your hands," Andres said.

Bev couldn't believe what she was hearing. All this time, the powerful magical person the queen's people had been searching for was Sheriff Rustin. And Rustin was really *the king!*

"And I suppose *you* were attracted to all this magic, eh?" Bev said, looking down at Biscuit before looking back at the duke. "What were you looking for in my kitchen, Bombadom? When Biscuit attacked you?"

He glanced at Andres. "I was looking for signs."

"Signs about what?" Bev asked.

"That your memory had returned," he finished softly.

"N-no, it hasn't," Bev said. "Why would it?"

"With the king coming back to his mind, I thought there might've been a trigger for you as well," Bombadom said.

"Me? Why me?" Bev took a step back, heart pounding. "Who…was I?"

Andres shared another look with Bombadom, but both turned to the king, who nodded. "You are the last surviving member of the King's Quartet, a powerful group of wizards who served and protected me," Ferilious said.

Bev swayed on her feet, the words making sense,

but at the same time, not. She was a wizard? Like Percival? It had been staring her in the face, but the idea was so far-fetched, she'd been trying her best to dismiss it entirely.

"That's impossible. I'm just... I don't have any magic," Bev said. "And Zed gave me a memory potion—"

"Zed's memory potion wasn't nearly powerful enough to undo the magic you'd cast on yourself," Bombadom said. "You were one of the most powerful wizards in our time. The spell was so all-encompassing, so complete, that it kept your identity a secret from a parade of visiting soldiers, some who should've recognized you immediately."

"But how did I end up here in Pigsend?" Bev asked.

Bombadom gestured to the king. "When the kingside fell, we needed to take precautions for our most valuable assets. His Majesty, of course, would be recognized by any senior member of Her Majesty's forces, so we changed his appearance, erased his memories, and installed him here under a real name with Dane to keep an eye on him. But even though you were less recognizable—"

"As your face wasn't on every coin in the kingdom," Andres said.

"—your magic was so powerful it could've been felt by anyone," Bombadom continued. "So you took a potion to forget who you were and forget that you even had magic. Broke your amulet. In the chaos of the fall, we lost track of you." He glanced at Rustin. "But it appears you knew to stay close to your king, even without your memories."

"I didn't stay in Pigsend because of Rustin," Bev said. "Wim McKee took me in, and to repay him, I worked a bit at the inn. I liked the people and the duties, so I decided to stay. I—"

She stopped, a vague memory flitting across her mind from those first few days. When she hadn't figured out what she was going to do, she'd been helping Wim McKee with laundry. Hendry had shown up, with Rustin in tow. She hadn't thought anything of it at the time, but was that…was that the reason she'd felt so at home in Pigsend?

She gazed across the group, many of whom she'd known for years now. "Did any of you know who I was?"

The Pigsend folks shook their heads, including Vellora. "I don't think I could've kept that from you, Bev."

"Did you come to town for Rustin, too?" Bev asked.

"No, I suppose it was fate that brought me here," she said. "And my beautiful wife who made me stay."

"You've got to tell her what's going on," Bev said. "She's worried sick about you. Are you going to just let her until whatever this is ends?"

"Until I'm sure she's not in danger of retaliation, yes," Vellora said. "She'll understand when we're through."

Bev swallowed. She couldn't quite believe what they were saying, even as all signs pointed to the truth. She looked down at Biscuit, who'd stopped wagging his tail and was staring up at her, with his lip curled under itself, almost like a snarl.

"And what about Biscuit?" Bev asked, before looking at Bombadom. "Was he my laelaps before? Is that why he was drawn to me?"

"I don't think he was anybody's," Bombadom said. "He was probably born after the war ended and was wandering the countryside. He sensed your magic and good heart—"

"Not to mention good food," Vellora added with a snort.

"And decided to stay," Bombadom finished. "He's quite the clever creature. He'll be a valuable asset—should you decide to join us."

"How come Zed didn't recognize me?" Bev asked. "Didn't he know me from battle?"

"I honestly don't know what he knows," Andres said. "Except he doesn't consider you a threat. If he thought you were truly one of the King's Quartet, he would've arrested you the moment he saw you."

"But you knew who I was," Bev said to Andres.

He nodded. "When Vellora introduced us, I recognized you immediately. But Vellora had described you as such a warm, friendly innkeeper, beloved in the community, and, most importantly, content with your life. I couldn't destroy that until I knew we were at the point of no return."

"Why now?" Bev asked. "It's been six years since the war ended."

"The war was difficult on everyone," Bombadom said. "We made some mistakes that cost us dearly. But the reality of living under Meandra's rule has sunk in for most people, and there's a feeling amongst the towns most severely under her thumb that the time is right for a change. Andres has been doing the work, talking with those in the outer villages like this, and he's amassed quite a following. We think Meandra's control is at her weakest now, especially with the way she's been bleeding the local towns dry."

"But you were the one demanding coin," Bev said, narrowing her gaze at Bombadom. "Were you doing that to convince the town that aligning with the king was the better move?"

"As I said, I was following orders," Bombadom said. "All the gold I collected is on its way back to Queen's Capital with one of Mackey's people. As much as it pained me to do, I have to keep up appearances, as you see." He smiled. "But now that His Majesty is back, I will return to Queen's Capital to continue spying on her until we are ready to execute our plan."

"A plan that would be much more apt to succeed if it included you," King Ferilious said. The voice that came from his lips sounded like Rustin, but it didn't. Perhaps the spell was still wearing off. "If you're willing to join us."

"I don't see how I can," Bev said slowly. "As I don't have any memories of anything you're talking about."

Bombadom pulled a vial from his pocket. "Would you like to?"

Bev had known this was coming. She finally had the answers she was looking for. She'd been one of the most powerful wizards in the land. She'd fought in the war. Perhaps been party to those mistakes Bombadom had spoken about. But for the past six years, she'd just been Bev: innkeeper, bread baker, sometimes mystery solver. She'd built herself a life here, had friends she'd do anything for, had a tidy business that she adored.

"I can't just…leave," Bev said softly.

"Would it help to know what's coming?" Bombadom asked. "Because my appearance here was just the first phase of the systematic destruction of rural towns just like Pigsend. The soldiers stationed to the south will stay here permanently unless they're pulled elsewhere by a pressing force. Anyone who hasn't paid their licensing fees and who doesn't have the proper precautions will be shut down, and…" He sighed. "Impressed into service."

"But why?" Bev said.

"Because she doesn't care for anyone else except herself," Ferilious said, his voice echoing across the space. "Believe me, I tried diplomacy with her. I tried to come to a solution without resorting to a war. But she declared it anyway. And she's deathly afraid of anyone with magic because she has none herself. All the magic she soaks up from towns like Pigsend goes into experiments to infuse her with it."

"She won't rest until Pigsend is wiped from the map," Bombadom said. "I've seen it happen time and time again."

"How can you be sure things will be different this time?" Bev asked. "How can you be sure you'll win?"

"We can't," Ferilious said. "But for the sake of your friends, your town, and your own life, shouldn't we at least try?"

Bev stared at the bottle in Bombadom's hand. They'd certainly painted a bleak picture, and she could tell herself that things would go back to normal—they always did—but Bombadom's face was deadly serious. He'd been in the queen's court. He knew, more than anyone else, what she was capable of. And the soldiers in the field to the south looked quite ensconced.

She thought of Lillie, living down in Merv's tunnel—which led her to worry about all the citizens in Lower Pigsend. What if the soldiers found the entrance? What if Nog couldn't get to the farmers' market—not that it mattered, because it was closed permanently. The people of Lower Pigsend would be back to square one, relying on Percival to fill all their needs. Until when? Until the old wizard died?

And what about Allen, with his pobyd magic, and Ida, with her dryad strength? Etheldra, with the tea-making ability, the Brewer twins.

PJ Norris, in Sheepsburg. How long until the queen's people came to *that* town and did the same thing? Would he even know to leave? Where could he go?

"If I take this potion," Bev started softly, "I'll remember everything? The good, the bad, the horrors, the joys...my own name?" She met Bombadom's gaze. "Will I forget who I've been?"

"No, the memories will sit together, as if you'd never lost your past," Bombadom said. "You'll still be you. Because, from what I understand, you've always been you. The person who signed up to join the kingside was motivated by the horrors she'd witnessed in the queen's country. She wanted to help people, to protect and serve those who couldn't protect themselves. I'm honestly not surprised to hear you've been the one saving the town and finding blackmailers and all the other wonderful things you've done this past year. You've always been you, Bev. Memories or not, that will never change."

The last bit of resistance fell away. The one thing she'd been most afraid of—besides reliving the horrors of war—was to find out she'd become an entirely different person as Bev. She had notions of a shadowy figure who'd hurt innocents and wielded magic without a care in the world.

She looked down at Biscuit, for one final confirmation. He wagged his tail and unfurled his tongue into a smile, an endorsement if ever she'd had one, and she turned to the others.

"Give me the potion."

Cheers erupted from the group, the sound so loud it scared Bev half to death. But it was joy, relief, and even Vellora was crying. Bombadom's face was beaming with happiness as he crossed the clearing and handed her the vial. She held it in her hand a moment, sensing that even touching it was the point of no return.

Then with a deep breath, she popped the top and downed it.

Warmth spread from her fingers to her toes to the ends of her very short hair. She smelled rosemary bread baking, the wafting aroma of a well-cooked beef roast, and a fresh cask of beer. But the sound that accompanied it wasn't Wim McKee. It was a younger woman with a smiling face looking down at her, and the hands maneuvering the dough were small and childlike. In front of her, a broom moved of its own accord to sweep up the tidy kitchen, and potions bubbled away on the stove.

"Now, Vebera, you'll want to knead it until the dough looks soft and pliable, like this." The soft voice filled Bev with so much longing and nostalgia that tears pricked her eyes—because she remembered what had happened to that voice, and what had happened to her small town, and why she'd decided to leave the queen's country and pledge her allegiance at sixteen to the king. She'd trained hard, fueled by the memories of her burning village, until she was the most powerful wizard she could be.

But there'd been mistakes. The Battle of Eriwall, where she'd seen blood on her hands, had shaken her to her core. She'd wanted to be *different* from the queen, but that battle had proven them all exactly the same. Guilt threatened to drown her.

And there was King Ferilious, standing in a small room with Bombadom and the man she now knew as Dane Sterling. The king downed a vial of potion, transforming into a figure she'd never seen before—but now knew to be Rustin.

Then Bev was in another room with Andres, and he held a potion in his hand.

"I won't remember anything?" her own voice, which sounded both foreign and familiar, was strained. "What if the king never comes back?"

"Then you'll live out the rest of your days in a quiet existence," he said. "Not a bad shake, in my opinion."

"Without my magic, though." The concept terrified her. How could she possibly do anything without it? "What if someone recognizes me?"

"They won't," Andres said. "You'll be as ordinary as I am."

"You aren't ordinary, Andres," she said with a chuckle.

He placed the vial in her hands. "The choice is yours. But this world is no longer safe for people like you, Vebera. And no matter how far you run, I don't think you'll be able to hide from the queen with your magic as it is."

It was true, and it filled her with pride and with dread. She'd worked so hard to be one of the most powerful wizards. And now she was about to throw it all away to hide with her tail between her legs as a normal villager in some small town.

"It's not fair that I should be able to forget what I've done," she said.

"By the very fact that you believe that," Andres said, closing her hand around the vial, "you deserve some peace. At least—"

Their conversation had been cut short. The queen's soldiers had found them, drawn by the aura of her powerful magic in a world that had been stripped clean of it. Should they get their hands on her, all would be lost.

So with a prayer that, one day, things would

return to normal, she'd downed the potion.

She opened her eyes in the present day, looking at faces that were familiar and *more* familiar to her. At the king, whose face filled her with a sense of immense pride. At Andres, with affection. Bombadom, too.

But she turned to Vellora and could still picture the day the soldier had come to town, the way she'd looked on her wedding day, and how scared she'd been when the blackmail letters had begun. At Freddie and Gore, the moment Gore's blackmail had been revealed. At Dane, and all the times he'd played with Sonny and Eldred in their musical trio. Andres, and the magical solstice. Shamus, and the way he'd sneered at her down in Lower Pigsend the first time. If only the wizard's apprentice had known who he was dealing with…

"How do you feel, Vebera?" Bombadom asked.

She looked down at her hands, tingling with magic. It felt like coming home, like finding Wim's things in the attic she'd forgotten about until stumbling across them by accident. Her power was immense, undeniable, and ready to be used.

"What's the plan?" she asked—then added with a smirk, "and call me Bev. I've grown rather fond of it."

Chapter Twenty~Two

Bev left Pigsend that very night, riding alongside her king and his most ardent supporters. Those with loved ones left behind wrote heavily coded letters that insisted they were all right but might not be back for a while. Bev sent one to Allen and Lillie, too, asking them to keep an eye on the inn and saying that she'd be back when she could. Ferilious's supporters made a ruckus in a town half a day's ride away so Zed's soldiers would be drawn from Pigsend, and that pressure would be alleviated.

The next several months were a whirlwind that would make quite the epic tale: full of angst and heartache, ups and downs, forward and backward movements, until finally the king was victorious against the queen. His first act was to restore the magical world as it had been before the queen changed everything. News spread quickly in the queen's country, but much slower in the rural countryside. In fact, when Bev and Vellora returned to Pigsend together, it seemed nothing had changed. But change would be coming.

Ida screamed when she saw her wife and threw herself into her arms, kissing her face wildly. Then, when she was done there, she grabbed Bev's face and kissed her cheeks.

"You two are in *so much trouble*!" Ida bellowed. "Leaving without saying a word. How *dare* you scare us all like that?"

Bev turned across the street, seeing her beloved inn for the first time in too long. But she couldn't go inside yet, as Allen and Lillie dashed across the street, tackling her to the ground and taking her to task for leaving them. Bev assured them she would give them the whole story but wanted to check on her inn first.

"We've kept it up for you. Lillie's been manning the desk and making the food," Allen said, finally letting Bev off the ground. "But goodness, Bev, where in the world have you been? There've been all kinds of rumors from travelers about the war restarting, and—"

"No need to worry about that," Bev said. She glanced at the sky—midday—and looked at Lillie.

"How's my dough looking? Already proofing?"

"It's a good thing you had that journal," Lillie said with a laugh. "I found it the day after you left, and it was invaluable."

Bev grinned. "Ol' Wim McKee doing the best to keep his inn running from beyond the grave."

"Bev, what happened to you? And why do you look…?" Allen swallowed. "I was so worried when you got hauled away in handcuffs."

"You got my letter, didn't you?" Bev said.

"Yes, but it seemed so… It's not like you to—"

"Let's all get inside," Bev said. "And I'll explain everything."

Lillie and Allen walked Bev into the inn, and she did a cursory inspection of the place. There were a few corners dustier than she would've liked, and the beds weren't made exactly as Bev did them, but overall, the inn was in fine shape, especially considering the way Bev had disappeared without a trace. She pressed her hand to the wall and silently apologized.

"I'm back now," she said, looking at the ceiling with a smile. "I hope I can regain your trust."

"Bev?" Allen and Lillie stood behind her. "What are you—"

"Beverage Wench!"

The front door swung open and a large, hulking figure waddled inside. Biscuit barked happily, his tail wagging as he ran over to sniff the moleman's feet.

"Merv!" Bev cheered. "How'd you know I was back?"

"Shamus appeared in my front room and demanded to be let back in to Lower Pigsend. He was telling a wild tale of epic battles and magical wizards and *defeating the queen*?"

Allen and Lillie spun to Bev, their eyes wide.

"Well, suppose I'll put on a kettle," Bev said with a sigh. "I've got a lot to fill you in on."

Bev, never one to sit still, broke out the rag and broom while she told the tale of Bombadom and Rustin's true identities, being whisked away to the other side of the country, and the epic battle between good and evil, magic and no, and how it all ended up with the queen and king. Merv, Lillie, and Allen sat listening with rapt attention, barely touching the tea Bev had set out, and didn't quite breathe until Bev finished her tale.

"So..." Lillie swallowed. "So we're allowed to live in the open? The queen's gone?"

"She's gone, but you know, these things take some time to work their way through the lands. There are mayors and sheriffs and registrars who might want to cling to power. Plus folks who'd gotten kind of used to not having magic around might not be too keen on it coming back. But the queen's people are no more, and we shouldn't see the likes of Karolina or Dag Flanigan darkening our door any time soon."

Allen swallowed. "What happened to my father?"

"He's fine," Bev said. "Sitting in a jail in the king's stronghold until they figure out what to do with him. Bombadom thinks there should be a little leniency for him, because he did have good intentions, even though he betrayed the kingside. Andres doesn't feel the same way, but that's up to them to figure out."

He nodded. "So what was your role in all this? Just swept up in it or...?"

Bev opened her mouth. She could tell them all about her true name, where she'd come from, how she was a powerful wizard who could make Percival's magic look like child's play, but...she didn't want to. In Pigsend, she wasn't the fearsome sole survivor of the King's Quartet. She was just Bev, the simple innkeeper, and she rather liked that life.

"You could say that," Bev said, smiling enigmatically. "In any case, I'm home now, so things can go back to normal."

~

News of the travelers' return spread like wildfire, and Bev entertained a steady stream of townsfolk, having to tell and retell the story multiple times to an ever-growing group of listeners. Allen, Lillie, and Merv, still too stunned that their dear friend was back and acting as if nothing had happened, stayed where they were, though Bev kept refilling their tea, just in case they remembered it was there.

Eventually, the front room hosted a crowd, including Etheldra, who'd been *most* offended that Lillie had been cooking, because it wasn't anything like Bev's, and Earl and Max, who'd cried and hugged her like she was their own daughter. Bardoff, who nervously decided to leave when Bev started talking about the queen's people losing, and the Brewer twins (who told Bev Vicky had gone back to Sheepsburg shortly after the soldiers departed, and she and the boys were doing fine). Apolinary and the Norrises, Alice Estrich, Herman Monday (who had, in fact, been at his house lying low when Bev had been taken). Trent Scrawl stood next to miller Sonny Gray (who was overjoyed to have one of his best customers back in town). Ramone Comely and their brother Horst stood in the corner holding hands. Even Rosie Kelooke and Wilda Murtagh came, standing in the corner and listening intently as Bev wove her tale. Through it all, she kept her true identity a secret, even from Mayor Hendry, who watched her with curiously pursed lips.

"Well, it has been quite the ordeal for Lillie and Allen to keep up with the inn," Hendry said. "I'm glad to see you're back to work."

"Might be barley soup tonight," Bev said. "Somehow I don't think we'll see the butchers for a little while."

"That's no excuse," Etheldra said, coming to her feet. "It's been *months* since I've had your delicious roast beef, Bev, and I won't wait a minute longer."

"Darling—" Earl began.

"Don't *darling* me," Etheldra growled. "It's beef roast, or I riot."

Etheldra rose quickly and marched out the door, Earl hot on her heels.

"I'm so happy you're all right," Holly Norris said, rushing up to take Bev's hands. "And to hear… Is it true? Can people with magic live…without fear?"

"Yes," Bev said with a knowing smile.

Holly's eyes screwed up with tears of relief, and she rushed away to her husband, who thanked Bev with tears in his eyes as they disappeared through the door. Bev had to believe they'd be on their horses within minutes, on their way to PJ to tell him the good news in person.

"Gosh, Bev, it just hasn't been the same without you," Sonny said. "I mean, the bakers have done well, of course, but it's just good to see your face."

"I'm sure I'll be back to making bread soon enough," Bev said.

Trent and Herman said nothing, hugged Bev tightly, then left arm in arm.

"Suppose the Harvest Festival's over, so they're back to being friends," Bev said to Hendry, who approached next. "We are going to have another one, aren't we? I really am keen on winning first place this year. Hopefully, we won't have a judge who hates rosemary."

"Or who's secretly a kingside spy," Hendry said with a look. "Well, we'll just have to see. I confess my *long list* of missives from Queen's Capital has gotten quite small of late, so I've been hesitant to put anything on the books. But if what you say is true…" She smiled. "Then we might just get back to the Harvest Festival the way it was intended to be."

"Nothing would make me happier," Bev said.

"So that's it, then? You just run off, have an epic adventure you're only telling us half of, and come back to bake bread and tend to your inn?" Hendry asked with eyebrows raised. "Seems like you'd want to stay behind with the king and continue making the world a better place."

"There are plenty of folks who can do that," Bev said. "But only one Bev to tend to the Weary Dragon Inn."

"Suppose you're right. The summer months are coming, and I'm sure you'll get busy again. Goodness knows the inn needs its annual cleaning." Hendry looked around then spotted Biscuit on the floor. "Oh. I see that's back."

"And very happy to be," Bev said. "It's good to see you, Jo." Hendry turned to leave, but Bev called her name once more. "Did you know about Rustin?"

"Whatever magic had been cast on him was powerful enough to fool me," Hendry said with a chuckle. "Though I confess I didn't really look too hard. Quite ingenious of those kingside folks to hide him like that. I don't think anyone had any clue." She eyed Bev. "Seems to be a common theme."

Bev smiled, holding up her hands. "I'm just a simple innkeeper."

"So you've said."

Before Hendry could leave, the front door swung open, and Ida came marching in, looking quite disheveled and carrying a large piece of beef.

"Etheldra was *insistent*."

~

Bev certainly couldn't say no to Etheldra, so she set to making dinner. Lillie had already begun the day's rosemary bread, so all Bev had to do was pop the loaves in the oven. The farmers who'd come by had brought crates of potatoes and carrots and other winter produce, and Bev chopped the vegetables up to cook alongside the beef. She wasn't sure how many to expect but based on the conversations still happening out in the front room, she erred on the side of making more than she needed.

Mid-afternoon, Lillie came by with a large cake, decorated with sugar frosting and a little magical sparkle on top. She placed it on the kitchen table and grinned at Bev.

"If I'm allowed to live in the open," she said, a

little nervously, "might as well do something fun."

"It looks decadent," Bev said. "And the bread is well done, too. I certainly owe you one."

"No, I still owe you," Lillie said, her eyes shining. "And it sounds like I owe you more, too, don't I? Because you've certainly done more than you've let on to help people like me live in the open."

"I'm not saying any more than I have," Bev said, getting back to her potatoes.

"I think...I'm sending that letter to Mr. Abora," Lillie whispered. "Goodness, I've been wanting to, but I didn't want to leave until you got back. I knew you would come back, of course. But I've really been thinking..."

"It's time," Bev said with a nod. "The world's changing again. Seems like a good opportunity to make a fresh start in a new town."

"I hope you don't mind, but I've made a little recipe book to take with me," Lillie said. "Mostly my recipes, but I did...well, I took your rosemary bread recipe. And Allen's mom's wedding cookies."

"Hopefully, you can make them for someone who actually gets married this time," Bev said with a chuckle. "Honestly, I'm happy for you, Lillie. But you'd better write me, or I may just have to come down to Silverkeep and bother you myself."

"Hear, hear!" Merv appeared in the doorway to the kitchen. "I can't believe you're going to leave without saying goodbye!"

"I'm not leaving *now*, Merv, just sending the letter," Lillie said, a little bashfully. "I hadn't a clue you were still here, or—"

"I'd gone home, but there's a steady stream of visitors in my front room, so it was absolutely unbearable. I'm here to rent a room until the chaos dies down."

"Of course," Bev said, wiping her hands and walking out to grab the guest book from the front room. As expected, there was still a crowd milling about, so Bev was happy she was making more food than usual. She brought the guest book back into the kitchen and flipped it to the first blank page. "Room one's available, right, Lillie?"

She nodded. "Yes, it is. And I'll be sure to bring you something delicious in the morning."

"Looks like there's something delicious right there," Merv said, nodding to the open kitchen door, where the cake was still visible. "Might I have a slice?"

"Oh, I think Lillie wanted to save it for dinner —" Bev began, but Lillie swept the cake from the table, cut a slice, plated it, then spun her hands around the remainder, which closed in on itself, though it seemed the cake had gotten smaller overall to compensate for the missing slice.

"Here you go," Lillie said, holding the plate to Merv. "Enjoy."

He stuffed the entire slice into his mouth and sighed happily. "Yes, that hits the spot. Outrageous. It really *has* been too long since you've come to visit me, Lillie."

"I was there just two days ago."

"And now you're moving *away*!" he moaned unhappily. "Whatever will I do?"

"Allen's able to use magic now," Lillie said. "I'll be sure to tell him to go hog-wild when he brings you goodies."

"I'm sure we're all in for a real treat, then," Bev said with a smile.

Dinner was served promptly at six, and the Weary Dragon hadn't been so full in months, if Lillie was to be believed. Bev could barely eat her own food, as everyone wanted to hear the tale of her adventures with the missing king over and over again. The meal went late into the night, until finally Bev had to tell everyone to go home.

"I've got to get my bread dough started," she insisted. "You all are welcome to come back tomorrow."

The guests departed, though Earl, Etheldra, and Max stayed behind to help Bev do the dishes. They insisted, wanting to spend more time with her, and she was grateful for the help. It had been quite a long day traveling, and she was ready to sleep in her own bed for the first time in months.

But first, after bidding farewell to the trio, she

gathered flour, water, rosemary, and salt, along with the leftover dough from yesterday, and got to work. After all, the business of the Weary Dragon didn't end just because its innkeeper had discovered something new about herself and had gone on an epic adventure. And she really was keen on winning first place at the Pigsend Harvest Festival this year.

"Nice to be home, eh, Biscuit?"

The laelaps snored in response.

Lillie the Pobyd begins her adventures in

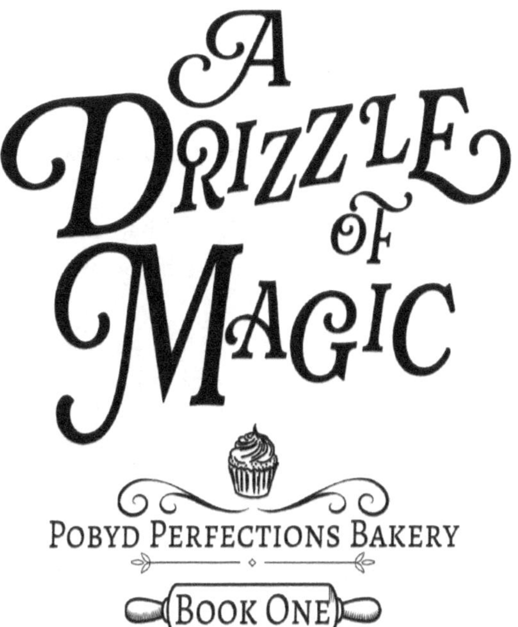

Acknowlegments

As always, first thanks goes to my husband, for supporting me, believing in me, and being my rock during the difficult season of two very small children and me trying to take on the world. Thanks must also go to my parents, my in-laws, and my aunt for being the world's best village and allowing me to keep writing with said very small children.

Thanks to Chelsea, Danielle, Lisa, and Lacey for being the all-star team who helps bring these beautiful books to life.

Thanks go to the Sush Street Team for being the cheerleaders who love these books and continue to read everything I put out.

And finally, and most ardently, thanks to you, the reader, for buying, loving, and sharing my cozy little story about Bev and her adventures. I'm so grateful I stumbled into this wonderful niche, and that it's brought you as much joy as it's brought me.

EMPATH

Lauren Dailey is in break-up hell, but if you ask her she's doing just great. She hears a mysterious voice promising an easy escape from her problems and finds herself in a brand new world where she has the power to feel what others are feeling. Just one problem—there's a dragon in the mountains that happens to eat Empaths. And it might be the source of the mysterious voice tempting her deeper into her own darkness.

Empath is a stand-alone fantasy that is available now in eBook, Paperback, and Hardcover.

About the Author

S. Usher Evans was born and raised in Pensacola, Florida. After a decade of fighting bureaucratic battles as an IT consultant in Washington, DC, she suffered a massive quarter-life-crisis. She found fighting dragons was more fun than writing policy, so she moved back to Pensacola to write books full-time. She currently resides there with her husband and kids, and frequently can be found plotting on the beach.

Visit S. Usher Evans online at:
http://www.susherevans.com/

www.ingramcontent.com/pod-product-compliance
Lightning Source LLC
Chambersburg PA
CBHW031646100726
47898CB00006B/1998